W9-AOR-856

3 4604 91037 3322

j Nay Large Print
Naylor, Phyllis Reynolds.

A spy among the girls [large
print]

W/D

A Spy
Among
the Girls

*Also by Phyllis Reynolds Naylor
in Large Print:*

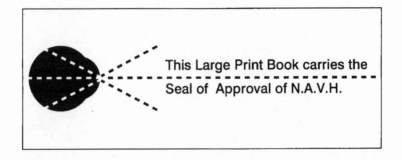

This Large Print Book carries the
Seal of Approval of N.A.V.H.

Boys–Girls Battle Series

A Spy
Among
the Girls

Phyllis Reynolds Naylor

SALINE DISTRICT LIBRARY
555 N. Maple Road
Saline, MI 48176

Thorndike Press • Waterville, Maine

Copyright © 2000 by Phyllis Reynolds Naylor

All rights reserved.

Published in 2003 by arrangement with Random House Children's Books, a division of Random House, Inc.

Thorndike Press® Large Print Middle Reader

The tree indicium is a trademark of Thorndike Press.

The text of this Large Print edition is unabridged. Other aspects of the book may vary from the original edition.

Set in 16 pt. Plantin by Elena Picard.

Printed in the United States on permanent paper.

Library of Congress Cataloging-in-Publication Data

Naylor, Phyllis Reynolds.
    A spy among the girls / Phyllis Reynolds Naylor.
        p. cm. — (Boys-girls battle series ; #6)
    Sequel to: A traitor among the boys.
    Summary: Are Beth and Josh really in love or just pretending to be in order to spy and continue the feud between the Malloy sisters and the Hatford brothers?
    ISBN 0-7862-5821-7 (lg. print : hc : alk. paper)
    1. Large type books. [1. Brothers — Fiction. 2. Sisters — Fiction. 3. Valentine's Day — Fiction. 4. Large type books.] I. Title.
PZ7.N24Sp 2003
    [Fic]—dc22   2003056172

For Michael Horwitz

Contents

One

Violins

Beth was in love, and it was positively sickening, Caroline thought.

Beth drew little hearts on the corners of her notebook, with the initials *B + J*. She lingered at the end of the footbridge each morning on the way to school, hoping that the Hatford boys would be leaving about the same time and she could walk to school with Josh. Worst of all, Beth acted as though she'd rather be with Josh Hatford than with her own sisters.

Caroline, age nine, was the youngest of Coach Malloy's three daughters. Eddie, the oldest, couldn't be bothered. At eleven, all she wanted was, number one, to think up a really good experiment for the sixth-grade science fair, and number two, to make the Buckman Elementary baseball team when tryouts were held the following month. If Beth, a year younger, wanted to act like a lovesick idiot, that was her problem.

"But, Eddie, it ruins everything! We were having such a wonderful time annoying the guys! We weren't supposed to fall in *love* with them!" Caroline protested as they ate their cereal and watched the sun trying to rise in a gray February sky.

Fog cut the West Virginia hills around Buckman in half, hiding the tops completely. It covered sections of the valley as well. From the kitchen window, the girls could see the swinging footbridge over the Buckman River, but they couldn't see the Hatfords' house on the other side.

"What do you mean, 'we'? *I* haven't fallen in love with anyone," Eddie told her, shaking the last of the Cheerios into her bowl.

"Good!" said their father, who had coached the college football team the previous fall and helped it make the playoffs. Now he was teaching chemistry. "Because I won't know till summer whether I'm leaving Buckman or staying. And if we move back to Ohio, I don't want a bunch of weeping daughters crying over leaving their boyfriends."

"Ha!" said Eddie. "Not on your life!"

Beth entered the kitchen at that mo-

10

ment. She had pulled her blond hair up on either side of her head, fashioned the top into curls, and fastened it using a large comb with daisies.

"Oh, brother!" Eddie said when she saw her. "Who are *you* supposed to be? Miss America?"

"Eddie, don't make fun of your sister," Mrs. Malloy said sharply as she set a plate of toast on the table. "Beth spent a lot of time on her hair, and I think she looks lovely."

"All for Josh," Caroline remarked.

"Pardon me while I gag," said Eddie.

"For your information, I just wanted a new look," Beth said, avoiding their eyes and quickly reaching for the butter.

"Yeah, a new look in nail polish too," Caroline said, grabbing one of Beth's hands to look at her nails, which Beth had painted purple to match her sweater. Each nail had a little *J* painted on it with sparkling silver.

"That's enough!" said Mrs. Malloy. "Everyone's entitled to a little privacy. Caroline, finish your toast, please."

All because Beth and Josh were in that play together where they had to hold hands! Caroline thought later as she brushed her teeth. But she had to admit what was really

11

bothering her. It wasn't that Beth liked Josh Hatford. Of the four Hatford brothers — Jake, Josh, Wally, and Peter — Josh was one of the nicest. It was the fact that by falling in love, Beth, not Caroline, was in the spotlight these days, and Caroline herself was used to being the center of attention.

If *she* were falling in love, she would make up a whole story to go with it. She would act out her own scenes, write her own love letters, and have secret meetings with her beloved down by the footbridge. Since she wanted to be a Broadway actress, she needed all the life experiences she could get, and falling in love was one of them. *Beth's* falling in love didn't count.

When it was time to leave for school, Caroline and Eddie left together because, these days, Beth always found excuses to lag behind. The Buckman River flowed into town on one side of Island Avenue, looped around the end, and came flowing back on the other side. A road bridge connected the end of Island Avenue to the business-district, but a swinging footbridge on one side provided a shortcut for the girls to College Avenue and to Buckman Elementary.

This morning, as Caroline and Eddie

were crossing the footbridge, looking down on the river's patches of ice heaped with snow like meringue on a pudding, they saw the Hatford boys already leaving their house, heading up the street toward school.

Eddie snickered. "Won't *that* put Beth in a snit," she said. "She purposely dawdled just so she could walk to school with Josh, and Josh started off early without her."

But Jake, Josh's twin, was first in line, plodding through the snow with seven-year-old Peter at his heels. Behind him came Wally, and Josh seemed to be hanging back. Every now and then he glanced over toward the Malloys' house, then quickly faced forward again.

In the next instant Beth's footsteps came tripping over the boards of the footbridge behind Caroline.

"Excuse me," Beth said, hurrying past, and caught up with Josh on the sidewalk, where he was pretending to tie his boot.

Caroline stopped walking and surveyed them from the bridge, hands on her hips.

"They aren't any good at all at falling in love," she declared. "When you fall in love, violins are supposed to play and bells are supposed to ring. A girl is supposed to rush across a bridge and into the arms of

13

her boyfriend. She's not supposed to pretend she just happened to meet up with him, and he's not supposed to pretend he stopped to tie his boot."

"I wouldn't know," said Eddie. "And the last thing I want making noise around me is violins."

But following along behind Beth and Josh, seeing how the sleeves of their jackets hardly even touched, much less their hands, Caroline made a decision: if she was ever going to know what it felt like to fall in love, she'd have to do it herself — so if she was ever asked to play the part of a woman in love, she could do it from the heart.

She would simply have to choose a boy and fall in love with him, and since the only boy who sat close to her in school was Wally Hatford — who sat directly in front of her, in fact — Wally Hatford it would be.

Two

Three Little Words

Wally couldn't believe what was happening. If his eyes didn't deceive him, one of the Hatford boys was falling in love, and he wasn't the one. It wasn't Jake, either, and it certainly wasn't Peter. All because Josh had held hands with Beth Malloy in a stupid play!

Things had not been the same since their best friends, the Bensons, had moved to Georgia and the Malloys had taken over their house. Things were not only different, they were weird. *None* of the Hatford boys had been in love before, and Wally hoped it would never happen to him. Josh never talked about Beth. He never even mentioned her name. But how many times could a guy stop to tie his boot on the way to school just so a girl could catch up with him? How many times could he forget his notebook so that he had to go back? Somehow Josh always managed to end up walking beside Beth Malloy.

Wally hung his coat outside the fourth-grade classroom and thought some more about love. He supposed he would fall in love someday whether he wanted to or not, because he was just an ordinary boy, and ordinary people usually fell in love at some time in their lives.

He was, in fact, the most ordinary person he knew. He wasn't fat, he wasn't thin; he wasn't short, he wasn't tall; he wasn't especially smart, but he wasn't stupid, either. And he wasn't a bit like Caroline Malloy, who should have been only in third grade but, because she was "precocious," had to be in *his* classroom. In the seat directly *behind* him, in fact.

Wally hung around the hall as long as he could, talking to his buddies. He had learned several things since starting fourth grade with Caroline: (1) Stay out in the hall as long as possible before taking your seat; (2) Don't speak to Caroline unless you have to; (3) Never lean back in your seat until Miss Applebaum has started the lesson: once class began, Caroline usually behaved herself, but until then, Wally could expect a poke in the back with a ruler or pen — Caroline's way of saying "Good morning."

He took his seat, leaning as far forward as possible, bracing himself for the sharp edge of a ruler or the prickly point of a pen. But nothing happened. He didn't even hear "Good *morning*, Wally!" There was no sound at all.

Miss Applebaum was talking about the month of February and how Americans celebrated two presidents' birthdays in that month. She talked about how students wouldn't remember *every*thing they learned in history, but she hoped they would learn enough so that when a famous person's name was mentioned, each student would remember at least *some*thing that person had done.

Still no poke in the back. Wally began to wonder if Caroline was there. Had he actually seen her when he sat down? Maybe she was absent. Maybe Miss Applebaum had switched seats around and Caroline was sitting somewhere else.

He slowly turned his head and glanced behind him. There was Caroline, all right, smiling the strangest smile he had ever seen, with all her teeth showing and her eyelids half closed. Wally jerked back around again, facing forward. Now, what kind of a smile was *that?*

"Let's hear some other famous names

17

and what you remember about them," said Miss Applebaum.

"Alexander Graham Bell; the telephone," said someone.

"Good, Bobby!" said the teacher.

"Orville and Wilbur Wright; the airplane," said someone else.

The names came faster.

"Laura Ingalls Wilder; *Little House on the Prairie*."

"Michael Jordan; basketball."

"Babe Ruth; baseball."

"Florence Nightingale; nursing."

"Rosa Parks; desegregation."

"Excellent!" said Miss Applebaum, looking pleased. "Caroline, did I see your hand?"

"Antony and Cleopatra," said the voice behind Wally.

There was a pause. "Yes?" said the teacher.

"Love," said Caroline.

And Wally wasn't sure why, but it felt as though a tray of ice cubes were sliding down his back.

Josh walked home with Beth again that afternoon, and he even stood at the end of the swinging bridge for five minutes talking to her.

Jake watched disgustedly from the porch,

and when his twin brother came up the walk at last, Jake, Wally, and Peter followed him inside.

"*What?*" Josh asked, looking from one brother to the next as they stared at him accusingly.

"Why did you have to go and do that?" Jake barked.

"Do *what?*" asked Josh, looking uncomfortable.

"Fall in love with Beth Malloy," said Wally.

"Who said we're in love? We're just friends, that's all," Josh argued.

"I'll bet!" said Wally. "You walk home with her every chance you get."

"You talk to her all the time," said Jake.

The phone rang and Wally answered. It was their mom, calling from the hardware store where she worked, wanting to make sure the boys had got home okay and that an ax murderer wasn't lurking there in the living room.

"Everyone's okay except Josh," Wally told her. "He's in love."

"Tell him to take two aspirin and talk to me in the morning," Mrs. Hatford joked. And then, "There are a few pieces of pizza left in the fridge. You guys can have those, but don't eat anything else or you'll spoil your appetite for dinner."

Wally hung up and turned again to face Josh, who had already found the pizza and was heating it in the microwave. "Mom said to take two aspirin."

"What?" said Josh. *"Why?"*

"I don't know. That's what she said."

Seven-year-old Peter was sitting at one end of the table, still wearing his coat, carefully unfolding a small piece of paper that seemed to have been folded a hundred times.

"What's that, Peter?" Jake asked.

Peter shrugged. "I don't know. Just something I found on the playground." He went on unfolding it, and the piece of notebook paper grew larger and larger. The boys watched as they waited for the microwave to ding.

When the wrinkled paper was smoothed out in front of him, Peter studied it a moment, then read aloud, " 'Beth loves Josh.' "

Josh instantly colored.

"See? *See?*" yelled Jake.

"That's not even her notebook paper. It's the wrong size," Josh said quickly.

"You even know the size of her notebook paper?" Wally croaked.

"She's *not* my girlfriend!" Josh bellowed.

"That paper's probably a joke. You guys don't know what you're talking about. I'm just hanging around Beth because . . . because . . . well, actually, I'm spying on them."

Jake and Wally were surprised. Josh's face was still pink.

"I'm just trying to find out what the girls are up to," Josh went on. "You should be *thanking* me, that's what."

"Well, why didn't you tell us before?" asked Jake, looking doubtful.

"Yeah," said Wally. "So what did you find out?" He was still worried. Those three little words, *Beth loves Josh,* were scary.

"Oh, nothing important yet, but if they're planning any kind of tricks on us, she'll tell me, you can bet."

"Yeah, but how can you be sure *Beth* isn't in love with *you?*" asked Jake.

"Don't be nuts," said Josh.

Peter was still studying the wrinkled piece of paper. "What does *X-X-X-X-X, O-O-O-O-O* spell?" he asked.

Three

Love

Caroline lay in bed the next morning thinking about all the things she needed to experience to become a really great actress. Joy, anger, fear, and sorrow. Happiness and tragedy, she decided.

The problem was that her life had been mostly happy up to this point. The worst thing that had ever happened to her was being sick the night of the community play and not getting to say her lines, but she'd been so sick she could hardly remember it.

Anger? She'd been angry at the Hatford boys, but she *enjoyed* being angry, so that didn't much count.

Fear? Well, she'd been sort of afraid when the Hatfords had locked her in the cellar of Oldakers' Bookstore.

What she had *not* experienced was a great tragedy or a great love, and she wondered how to go about falling in love with

Wally Hatford. More to the point, how to make Wally Hatford fall in love with *her.*

She would dress with care that morning because, she decided, you can't expect someone to fall in love with you if you don't look your best. She put on black tights, a black skirt, and a red sweater with little black sheep all over it.

When she went down to breakfast, she asked, "Mother, how did you make Dad fall in love with you?"

Mrs. Malloy turned around from the stove, where she was making pancakes, and stared at her youngest daughter. "Sweetheart, you can't *make* anybody love you. It just has to come naturally."

Coach Malloy looked up from his newspaper and took another sip of coffee. "It was witchcraft," he said. "Seductive glances, a dulcet voice, shining hair, sparkling eyes . . ." He and Mrs. Malloy smiled at each other.

"Who are *you* trying to make fall in love with you?" Eddie asked, pouring the raspberry syrup. "If one more person in this family falls in love, we'll all go nuts. Beth's moping around is bad enough. Don't you start, Caroline."

But Caroline rather liked the thought of it. She imagined a play on Broadway titled

Caroline in Love. It would be romantic and funny at the same time, but it would end tragically. Caroline liked playing tragedy best of all. She was just about to ask her parents what great tragedy had ever happened to them when Coach Malloy suddenly gave a little whistle.

"What about this!" he said, staring at a newspaper story. "It says the abaguchie has been sighted again."

"The what?" asked Caroline. And then she remembered the strange animal that had been glimpsed now and then around Buckman. Since no one knew what it was, someone had nicknamed it the abaguchie.

"The creature who stole the Thanksgiving turkey off the Hatfords' back porch," Eddie reminded her. "Where did they see it this time, Dad?"

"A man was out gathering firewood along the river last week, it says, and claims he saw just a glimpse of the animal from a distance," Coach Malloy told them, scanning the page. "It was a tawny color, but certainly not a dog, he claims."

"Something else to worry about!" said Mrs. Malloy.

Beth came into the kitchen just then and announced that she was reserving the kitchen the day before Valentine's Day because she was going to make a double-chocolate frosted heart for Josh.

"Oh, brother!" said Eddie.

"Sounds wonderful," said Coach Malloy. "Would you consider making one for your dad, too? I could do with a double-chocolate frosted heart." He grinned.

Beth smiled. "I'll think about it."

"Just don't put it out on the porch to cool or the abaguchie might get it," said Caroline.

"It's back?" asked Beth.

"Just once I'd like it to stick around long enough for somebody to get a really good look at the beast and tell what it is," Coach Malloy said. "No one's seen more than its tail and a flash of color. The sheriff says his best guess is a bobcat."

"Whatever, I want you girls to stay out of the woods for a while," said their mother.

When Caroline went upstairs to brush her teeth, she imagined Wally Hatford rescuing her from the clutches of the abaguchie. Or even her rescuing Wally. She decided that if Wally was going to fall in love with her, perhaps she ought to give *him* a valentine — a really gorgeous valentine. If he gave her one in return, she decided, she could claim she'd experienced love. If he didn't, at least she would know what rejection felt like, and she could call it a tragedy.

At school, however, Wally was proving more difficult than she had imagined. She hadn't even told him yet that she was going to fall in love with him, but he was leaning about as far forward, away from her, as he could get.

When she tapped him, very gently, on the shoulder before class, he didn't even turn around.

"*What?*" he said. Not very pleasantly, either.

"I just wondered if you'd noticed my new sweater," Caroline said sweetly. "I wore it just for you."

Wally's back seemed to stiffen and his ears turned pink.

"Why?" was all he said, and he still didn't turn around.

Caroline stood up and leaned way over her desk until her mouth was right by Wally's left ear. "Because I think I'm falling in love with you, Wally," she whispered, as softly and sweetly as she knew how.

Wally Hatford rose straight out of his seat and asked permission to use the rest room, and Miss Applebaum looked at

Caroline strangely. Caroline just smiled innocently and tried to imagine how an actress would act out the part of someone dying because of a broken heart.

That afternoon the class voted on whether or not to have a Valentine's party. The sixth-graders had already voted no. The fifth grade voted no just to be like the sixth grade, but when the fourth grade realized that there would be no punch and valentine cookies and chocolate hearts without a party, they voted yes.

"There's one rule, however," Miss Applebaum said. "You don't have to give out any valentines at all if you don't want to, but if you do, you can't leave anyone out. If you want to give valentines just to girls, you have to give one to every girl. If you want to give only to boys, you have to give one to all the boys. This isn't a popularity contest."

Great. Just great, thought Caroline. She had already planned to give some crazy valentines to the girls in her class, but she wanted to give a valentine to only one boy, namely Wally. Well, she'd just give her valentine to Wally after the party was over, that was all. There was no rule that said she couldn't hand a boy a valentine out in the hall. But Wally would get the biggest, most beautiful valentine she could find.

After school she walked down to the business district to Oldakers' Bookstore and looked over the rack of valentines. There were funny cards, serious cards, valentines for mothers, fathers, brothers, sisters, aunts, uncles, and grandparents. But it wasn't until Caroline looked in the sweethearts' section that she found just the right valentine for Wally, just the kind to get him to fall in love with her.

It was the largest card on the rack, with a big red satin heart in the middle, surrounded by a ruffle of white lace.

To the man of my dreams, it said on the card. And a verse on the inside read:

> *My sun, my moon; my stars, my air;*
> *The music I hear everywhere.*
> *My summer, fall; my winter, spring;*
> *Darling, you're my everything.*

Four

Tracks

Wally decided to stay as far away from Caroline as possible because she was acting positively weird. Her walk was crazy, her talk was crazy, and her smile was craziest of all. She followed him around the playground at recess and tried to sit at his table at lunch. He simply surrounded himself with friends and didn't go anywhere if his buddies weren't with him.

It was a relief each day to get home and away from her. A relief that it was February, and cold. He didn't have to go outside much, so he didn't risk running into her that way. The only cloud on the horizon was Valentine's Day. Valentine's parties always made him a little nervous, but he wasn't going to give valentines to anyone this year, not even the boys, so he told himself to quit worrying about it. All he had to do at the party was eat candy and cookies and watch the other kids go around dropping cards into homemade valentine boxes. Big deal.

He was sitting on the couch with Peter one evening, eating a bag of corn chips, when Josh walked by and said, "Hey, Wally, I want to use your room for a while. Okay?"

Wally popped another corn chip in his mouth, thought for a moment, and asked, "What for?"

"Just something private. Okay?"

"Okay," said Wally, but he couldn't imagine what. Josh and Jake had their own room, after all, and Josh had never asked to use Wally's room before. Wally and Peter went on watching TV and sharing the corn chips, and then Wally said what he was thinking: "I wonder what he wants it for?"

"Probably to spy," said Peter, thrusting one hand into the corn chips sack.

Wally looked at Peter. "Why do you think that?"

"It's what he said he was going to do, isn't it? Spy on the girls?"

Wally frowned. It might make sense if Wally's bedroom were at the front of the house, where possibly, if you used binoculars, you could get a good view of the house across the river where the Malloys were staying. But Wally's bedroom faced

30

the backyard, so that made no sense at all.

A few minutes later Jake came by. "Have you seen Josh?" he asked.

Wally couldn't think of what to say. If Josh had wanted Jake to know what he was doing, he would be doing whatever he was doing in their bedroom, not Wally's.

"He's spying," said Peter.

"What?" said Jake.

"Yeah, that's probably what he's doing — spying on the girls," said Wally.

"Well, heck! Why didn't he tell me?" Jake muttered, and went on out to the dining room.

A half hour later, after Peter had gone out to the kitchen for ice cream, Wally went upstairs and tried to open the door to his room. The door wouldn't budge, even though there was no lock on it. It felt as though someone had his feet braced against it.

"Who is it?" came Josh's voice softly.

"It's me," Wally whispered back.

"What do you *want?*"

Wally thought about it. To get into his room, of course. "To . . . to get my socks," he blurted out.

"What do you mean? You've already got your socks. Go away. I'll be through after a while," Josh told him.

Wally went back downstairs and wished he hadn't done that. He liked it when Josh confided in him. Usually Josh and Jake did everything together and had their own secrets. He wanted his brother to know he could trust him.

He wandered through the downstairs. Peter was eating ice cream in the kitchen, Mr. Hatford was in the living room watching the news, Mrs. Hatford was working a crossword puzzle at one end of the dining room table, and Jake was doing homework at the other end.

"As soon as Josh comes in, tell him to come out here and help me with our math assignment," Jake said. "He must have done his already."

"Okay," said Wally.

"Where *is* Josh?" asked Mrs. Hatford.

"Around somewhere," Wally answered, wandering off again.

He went upstairs and sat down on the top step, studying the wallpaper. It was a striped paper of gray and green, a green rope twisting round and round a gray column, with skinnier lines on either side. All around the hall and down the stairs, columns and columns of gray with green rope twisting around them as far as Wally could see.

He lay down and looked at the stripes from the floor. Now they were horizontal stripes, one on top of the other, all over the wall. Who designed wallpaper? Wally wondered. He liked to think about things like that. Were there factories where artists sat around at drawing boards, designing gray stripes with green ropes around them, and purple stripes with blue ropes around them, and brown stripes with yellow? Did they have to go on drawing the same pattern with every color you could think of before they could draw something new?

How did you know you wanted to design wallpaper when you grew up? Wally tried to think of all his friends — the Benson boys in particular — and the things they had talked about being when they grew up. Policemen, doctors, forest rangers, football players . . . He couldn't ever remember hearing someone say he wanted to design wallpaper.

The door to his room opened at last and Josh came out with an envelope under his arm. He looked surprised to see Wally waiting there on the stairs and went quickly into the room he shared with Jake.

"Thanks," he said.

"Jake's looking for you," Wally said.

"Okay," said Josh. He came out a moment later and went downstairs.

Wally opened the door to his room and turned on the light. He looked around. He didn't see any binoculars. No false mustaches or other disguises. Nothing that looked like spy stuff. He peered all about — at the top of his bed, the top of his dresser — nothing.

He got down on his stomach and looked under his bed. There were some small scraps of white paper, a little scrap of pink, and some tiny red sparkles, the kind you might find on a cupcake. What the heck had Josh been doing? Making cupcakes? Wally sniffed the air. Nothing *smelled* like cupcakes.

"Wally!" came Mrs. Hatford's voice from downstairs. "You haven't done your chores yet. I wish I didn't have to remind you every night to empty the wastebaskets and take out the garbage."

Wally wished she didn't either. Jake and Josh usually remembered to do their chores because they did them right after dinner. One of them took the clean dishes out of the dishwasher and the other put the dirty ones in. You could hardly forget to do that with your mother watching you right there at the table.

Peter didn't get a chance to forget his

work either. He had to set the table for dinner every night. That was easy, because as soon as he got hungry, his stomach reminded him to set the table. But how could you remember to empty wastebaskets and take out the garbage when there were more important things to think about — like what was your brother doing in your room? Making cupcakes?

Wally picked up his wastebasket and took it around to the baskets in all the other bedrooms, dumping their contents into his. He did the same with the bathroom wastebasket, then went downstairs and began emptying trash from all the baskets there.

He went into the kitchen, pulled the garbage sack from under the sink, and took both the wastebasket and the garbage sack out the back door.

The moon was full, and the backyard was bright in the one inch of snow that had fallen that evening. It looked to Wally as though the backyard had been covered with cream cheese.

He went down the steps and started to open the lid of the garbage can, then paused, his hand in the air.

"Hey!" he called. And then more loudly, "Hey, Josh! Jake! Hey, Dad! Come here!"

A chair scraped against the floor inside the house, and there were footsteps. Then the back door swung open.

"What is it?" asked Jake. Josh stuck his head out too; then Mr. Hatford came out on the porch, followed by Peter.

"Look!" said Wally, pointing.

There on the ground, around the garbage can, were large paw prints in the snow. They were larger than a cat's. Larger than a dog's. And they certainly weren't deer tracks. They looked like nothing Wally had ever seen before.

"The abaguchie!" breathed Peter. "That's what it is."

Five

The Plan

Eddie was upset.

"All the good ideas are already taken!" she complained, telling the family about the science fair that was coming up at school. Each of the sixth-graders was to think of an experiment. "I had a good idea about photosynthesis: taken. I had another idea for evaporation: taken. Someone is even going to do that experiment on magnetism I did back in Ohio last year."

Mrs. Malloy was framing a picture to put at the top of the stairs. "Well, maybe you've got to think in a new direction, Edith Ann," she said. Eddie hated to be called by her full name. "Maybe you need to think of an experiment involving people instead of things."

"You mean, evaporate *people?*" Caroline asked incredulously from the living room couch.

"No, I mean . . . do a survey, maybe. Be creative! You'll think of something," Mrs. Malloy said.

"We're supposed to think up a hypothesis and then test it out," said Eddie.

"What's a hypothesis?" asked Caroline.

"You figure out something you think might be true, and then you set up an experiment to test it," Eddie explained. "I might say that plants always grow toward the light. That's what I think would happen, so that would be my hypothesis. Then I might put some plants in a box with a window on one side. I might keep them there for a week, and when I took the cover off the box, I'd expect all the plants to be leaning toward the window if my hypothesis was true."

"So, do that one," said Beth. "Everyone knows that plants lean toward the light."

"That's why I can't do it. It's dumb," said Eddie. "Even a *survey* would be better than that."

Mr. and Mrs. Malloy had a faculty dinner to attend that evening, so the girls were on their own. Eddie made spaghetti sauce, Beth boiled the spaghetti, and Caroline made the salad. As they were eating, Caroline said that all the boys wanted to talk about in her class that day was the abaguchie. Wally Hatford had told them he'd gone out to empty the garbage and there were strange tracks in the snow made by no creature known to man.

"Ha!" said Eddie. "I wouldn't believe a thing those Hatfords say."

"Some of the boys claim the abaguchie is a prehistoric animal," Caroline went on. "Boys are the most gullible creatures in the whole world. They'll believe anything."

"*Some* boys, maybe," said Beth.

"I'll bet if we said we had the abaguchie in our garage, every boy in school would be over to see it," said Caroline.

Eddie suddenly put down her fork and said, "Hypothesis: boys are more gullible than girls."

"True!" said Caroline.

"But I have to prove it," said Eddie, and Caroline could tell from the glint in her eye that Eddie's brain was racing on ahead of her. "What if we . . . I know! What if we spread the word on the playground that we've trapped the abaguchie in our garage, and if people want to see it, they should come by our house on Saturday or something."

"What you'd get would be huge crowds of kids coming together. You wouldn't

39

know who really believed it and who didn't," said Beth.

Eddie sat twisting a long strand of spaghetti around and around on her fork, her blond head resting on one hand. "Okay," she said at last, jerking upright. "Then the messages have to be secret. Each kid has to think he or she is the only one we invited and can't tell anyone else. We could put a note in the pocket of every coat hanging outside the classrooms from second to sixth grades. Any kid younger than seven probably wouldn't be able to read it."

"Yeah," said Caroline, "but once kids get to our house and there isn't any abaguchie to see, then what? We'll have a riot."

"Hmmm," said Eddie. She hadn't thought of that.

Caroline considered her sisters pretty lucky to have such a precocious child as herself in the family.

"We'll make up a picture of an abaguchie," said Eddie. "We'll cut parts of animals out of magazine pictures and paste them all together and claim that's what it looks like. I mean, 'abaguchie' is just a made-up name, right? So our picture will just be a made-up animal, and that's what we'll show anyone who comes over."

Dumb, dumb, dumb, thought Caroline.

Who was going to be satisfied with a picture of an abaguchie? And where did *she* fit into all this? Well, Caroline Lenore Malloy was going to play a part whether Eddie knew it or not. In fact, Caroline was going to save the day. She would *be* the abaguchie.

Beth and Eddie were still discussing the plan as though Caroline weren't even there. "But there are three hundred kids in school, not counting kindergarten and first grade. Who's going to write out three hundred messages?" Beth was saying.

"We'll do it on Dad's computer," Eddie told her. "I'll type up a message, then we'll copy it all down the page, and print a whole bunch of pages till we get three hundred messages. Then we'll cut the pages in strips."

"And if a parent gets hold of one of the slips of paper and tells our folks?" asked Beth.

"We'll just explain. It's a scientific experiment to see if boys are more gullible than girls. There's no harm in that."

Eddie didn't seem to care that kids would be disappointed, Caroline thought. As long as she got an experiment out of it, that was all that mattered. Well, Caroline would just have to see that no one

41

went away disappointed.

As soon as they'd finished eating, Eddie turned on the computer and typed out this message:

Private: This is a secret message. If you want to see the abaguchie, come to 611 Island Avenue between 3 and 4 p.m. to-morrow, Saturday. Free. Do not tell anyone about this message or you will not get in.

She copied it again and again all down the page, then printed out page after page, until there was a message for every student in the second through sixth grades.

Eddie and Beth took their scissors and cut the papers into strips, a message on each strip, then divided them up and stuck them in their book bags. After that, they spent the evening cutting parts of animals out of old magazines and pasting them together on a sheet of paper, until they had a weird animal that looked like no animal at all.

"This isn't any good," said Beth. "It's just plain stupid."

"Well, it's all we've got, so it will have to do," Eddie said irritably. "Meanwhile, I'll hide this under my bed. The folks will be in Morgantown on Saturday afternoon, and the experiment will be over by the time they get back. Not that I'm doing anything *wrong*, of course. I just . . . I don't know how Mom would feel about us luring kids over here thinking they'll see a real animal."

Caroline said nothing. Nothing at all.

The next morning, however, before the girls left for school, Eddie gave Caroline some of the messages to put in coat pockets. *Sure!* thought Caroline. *When there's work to be done, call on good old Caroline.* Still, she took her share of the slips of paper without complaining.

She didn't say a word to Wally. She was as good as gold all day. Eddie had already decided that the messages should be put into coat pockets after the last recess so that kids wouldn't be finding them and talking about them with their friends. Better that each student should read the message alone and decide for himself or herself whether or not to go see the abaguchie.

Caroline did her afternoon arithmetic lesson, wrote a paragraph for American history, and promptly at two-thirty-five went up to Miss Applebaum's desk with a rather urgent look on her face, one hand on her stomach, and asked to use the rest room. Miss Applebaum nodded and Caroline went out in the hall.

She could see Eddie coming out of her classroom far down one end of the corridor, and Beth in the hallway at the other end. Eddie disappeared into the south corridor, Beth disappeared into the north, and Caroline took a handful of slips from her sweater pocket and began putting them in the pockets of all the coats hanging outside her classroom. It was understood that Beth would fill the pockets of the second- and third-graders, Eddie would do the fifth and sixth grades, and Caroline would do the pockets of her fourth-grade class.

Caroline's heart was beating fast and her hands felt cold as she walked silently along the rows of coats, dipping one hand down into the pocket of her sweater. She knew she was taking an extra-long time, but she hoped Miss Applebaum would figure she had been feeling a little sick and needed extra time in the rest room.

The girls usually hung their coats on one side of the hallway, the boys on the other. On one side were purple, pink, and green nylon jackets, some with fake fur around the hoods, mittens with designs on them, and a few snow boots of blue and pink and purple.

On the other side of the hallway were brown and gray and blue and black coats, some of wool, some of nylon, and stocking caps stuffed up sleeves or flung this way and that on the rack.

Caroline finished putting messages in the girls' pockets and started down the other side of the hall. She put her hand deep into the pocket of a brown corduroy jacket with a sheepskin collar and didn't notice Wally Hatford walking out of the classroom toward the boys' rest room. She didn't see him stop and stare at her before continuing silently on his way.

Six

Spy Time

"Caroline Malloy steals," Wally announced to his brothers as they walked up to their porch that afternoon.

"How do you know?" asked Josh.

"I saw her in the hall today with her hand in a boy's coat pocket. She didn't see me, though."

"What did she take?"

Wally shrugged. "I don't know. She was probably looking for money or something. It was Kevin Miller's jacket."

Wally went inside and started to take off his coat. Then he remembered the quarter he'd found on the way to school that morning and wondered if it was still where he'd put it. If Crazy Caroline was going around checking pockets to see if there was any money in them, she'd undoubtedly taken his quarter too.

He thrust both hands in both pockets.

The quarter was still there. There was also a little slip of paper, which he pulled out with two fingers. While his brothers went into the kitchen to get a snack, Wally unfolded the paper and read:

Private: This is a secret message. If you want to see the abaguchie, come to 611 Island Avenue between 3 and 4 p.m. tomorrow, Saturday. Free. Do not tell anyone about this message or you will not get in.

What in the world?

Wally looked around to see if Josh or Jake had seen him reading the secret message. He wanted to go right out and show it to them, but maybe he shouldn't. That was the Malloys' address, all right, and Caroline had obviously put it in his pocket. Maybe *that* was what she'd been doing out in the hall. She'd sure been acting weird lately, as though she wanted Wally to be her boyfriend, and now maybe she liked Kevin, too. Well, that was fine with Wally. Kevin could have her all to himself.

Still, what did it mean? Was it possible the Malloys really had captured the strange animal that had been lurking around Buckman? Maybe Coach Malloy had trapped it in their garage and Caroline was

47

going to let Wally and Kevin have a first look at it because she liked them so much.

He stared at the note again. Why couldn't he tell anyone? he wondered. And how would they know whether he had or not? That was easy. Everyone he told would want to come too, and a whole crowd would show up at the Malloys'. No, he had to keep this secret and go alone. But if this was a trick . . .

He went into the kitchen, where Jake and Josh were getting down the crackers and peanut butter. Peter was on the phone talking to their mother. She always called to see if things were okay.

"We're all here and we're not murdered or anything," Peter told her.

When he hung up, they sat down at the table and passed around the crackers and orange juice, the peanut butter, and some cheese. But they all seemed unusually quiet to Wally. Jake and Josh would normally be jabbering away or quarreling about something, but now each of his brothers seemed to have something on his mind. Peter, in fact, was holding something tightly clasped in his left hand, and finally, when all the cheese was gone, he opened his fist, unfolded a little slip of paper, and asked, "What does *a-b-a-g-u-c-h-i-e* spell?"

Jake and Josh and Wally all paused with crackers in their hands and stared at Peter.

"Did *you* get one too?" asked Jake.

Josh turned to Jake. "What do you mean? Did *you* get one?"

"Then you got one, too?" Jake asked.

"We all must have got them," said Wally, relieved. "I'll bet Crazy Caroline was putting them in our pockets."

"What does it spell?" Peter asked again.

"Abaguchie," Wally told him. "But it's probably a big fat trick, Peter. She just wants us to make fools of ourselves."

"What if they really did catch something?" asked Josh.

"There's only one way to find out, and you're the official spy," Jake told him.

"Right!" Josh said quickly. "Leave it to me. I'll call Beth and say I'm coming over." He dialed the Malloys' three times, however, and each time the line was busy. Jake got tired of waiting and ambled upstairs. Then Peter left, and finally Wally. Josh continued dialing.

Wally stretched out on his bed and played a few games with his Game Boy, but when he came back down, Josh was still there.

"I thought you were going over to the

Malloys'," Wally said.

"I am. Her mom said Beth stopped by the library on her way home and should be back in half an hour. Why don't you walk over there with me, Wally? I mean, you don't have to come in or anything. But we could sneak around the garage first and see if they've got anything trapped in there. Look in their basement window, maybe, and see if the abaguchie's down there."

"Okay," Wally agreed. He didn't mind as long as he didn't run into Crazy Caroline.

And so, with Jake upstairs listening to CDs and Peter playing with his Matchbox car collection, Josh and Wally put on their coats and crossed the swinging bridge. They circled around the garage first, so that the girls couldn't see them coming, and tried to look inside. The door was closed, however. The windows of the basement were dark as well.

"If there *was* an animal over here, I'll bet it would be making a powerful lot of noise," said Wally.

"Yeah," Josh said. "I'll bet Caroline thought up this whole stupid thing herself. I'll bet Beth doesn't even know about it."

"Well, good luck," Wally told him.

"You don't want to . . . uh . . . wait out here or anything?" Josh asked.

"Why should I wait? You might be in there a long time," said Wally.

"Right," said Josh. He walked toward the back door of the house, and Wally went on down the hill to the swinging bridge.

Wally couldn't figure out whether Josh really was a spy, or whether he was in love with Beth, or neither. As he crossed the river, he decided that if he ever *did* fall in love with a girl, he'd get a friend to like her too, and then they could both go see her together. Then he wouldn't have to do all the talking.

As soon as he got into the house, Jake quizzed him. "Where have you guys been? Where's Josh?"

"Just snooping around the Malloys'," Wally said.

"Why didn't you tell *me?*"

Wally shrugged. "Somebody had to stay with Peter. Josh went inside their house, so I came on home."

"You hear anything? Like an animal trapped somewhere?"

"Nope. I think Caroline the Crazie thought this whole thing up herself. She's been really, really weird lately."

"Weird how? Weird mean or weird nice?"

"Weird weird," said Wally.

"Does she still poke you in the back?"

"No."

"Lean against you? Grab hold of your arm?"

"No! Of course not!" said Wally. "I can't explain it. She just acts goofy."

Jake sighed and sprawled out on the couch, one foot dangling over the end. "How did we get mixed up with these goofballs anyway?" he asked no one in particular. "You know, if we hadn't spied on the girls when they were first moving in, we could have totally ignored them and we wouldn't be having a thing to do with them now. We wouldn't have had any snowball fights, wouldn't have locked Caroline in the cellar at Oldakers'. We wouldn't have howled outside their window or got them lost in the woods or . . ."

"Or had any fun at all," put in Wally.

Jake looked over at him. "You don't want the Bensons to come back, do you?"

"What?" said Wally. "I never said that!"

"But you don't, do you?"

"Sure I do! Of course I do! I just . . . I'm not sure I want the Malloys to leave, that's all."

"I'm not sure either," said Jake. It was the very first time he'd admitted it.

Seven

A Visit Before Dinner

Beth had just put her books on the dining room table when there was a knock at the door.

"Oh, that's probably Josh," called her mother. "He phoned and said he'd be over."

"Over *here?*" Beth cried, her cheeks growing pink, and she ducked into the downstairs bathroom to brush her hair.

"He's coming to see *you*, not your hair," Caroline said. "Josh already knows you have hair."

The knock came again, and Beth answered. There stood Josh in his black-and-silver jacket, his dark hair windblown.

"Well . . . hi," Beth said. "Come on in."

"Were you busy or anything?" Josh asked. "You aren't having dinner or something?"

"No, we don't eat till Dad gets home,"

she told him, and led him through the hall into the living room. Then, because Eddie was sprawled on the couch reading the comics and Caroline was watching TV, Beth took him into the dining room and they sat somewhat awkwardly at the big table.

Caroline turned the sound down on the TV so that she could hear what they were saying.

"So what are you doing tomorrow?" Josh was asking Beth, and she seemed flustered.

Was he asking her out the next day? Caroline wondered. Was that any way to ask a girl to go somewhere with you? How was Beth going to tell him that, actually, she and her sisters had invited every kid from second to sixth grade over at three o'clock to see an abaguchie? That Josh wasn't the only one who had received the "secret" message?

"Well . . . I . . . um . . . I'm going to be busy all afternoon, I think," Beth said.

"All afternoon?" Josh said teasingly. "It won't take *that* long to show me the abaguchie, will it?"

Uh-oh, thought Caroline, and glanced over at Eddie on the couch. What was this, a spy among them? Eddie put down the comics and listened too.

"So what's the deal?" Josh insisted. He

just wouldn't quit. If Beth told him they wanted to see who was gullible enough to show up on Saturday, Josh certainly wouldn't come.

"Well, it's . . . it's sort of a project with my sisters," Beth said hesitantly. "It's going to take most of the afternoon."

"Homework? Something for school? Anything I can do to help?" Josh asked.

Eddie suddenly rose from the couch and went to the doorway. "As a matter of fact, Josh, there is," she said. "Since you're the best artist in school, it would really help if you'd draw a picture of what you think the abaguchie looks like."

Beth and Josh looked at each other, and Caroline came in from the living room. It was a great idea, because Josh had done the scenery last month for the community play, and if the girls could involve him in the experiment, maybe he wouldn't go around telling everyone what they were doing.

"The abaguchie is a *school* project?" Josh asked.

Eddie nodded.

"I thought you guys would know already what the abaguchie looks like. In fact, I thought you had it out there in your garage."

Caroline stared at Beth, who stared at Eddie, each wondering what to say.

"You kept the message secret, I hope," said Eddie.

"Peter told me you invited him too," Josh said. "He couldn't read the word *abaguchie*. Then Jake and Wally said *they* got invitations."

"I *knew* we shouldn't have given them to the second-graders," Beth said.

"Aha!" said Josh. "You invited the whole school? So what *are* you up to?"

Eddie looked helplessly at her sisters. There was nothing to do but let Josh in on the secret. Well, not *all* of it, perhaps. "Josh, it's really, really important that you not tell anyone what we're doing, because it's all part of my experiment for the science fair. We're going to keep a record of who shows up. Sort of a psychological study of second through sixth grades — how many kids come from each grade."

"You mean, who's dumb enough to believe you've got an abaguchie in your garage?" asked Josh.

"No, it doesn't have anything to do with smart or dumb."

"Who's the most *gullible*," said Caroline.

"But if you go around telling people it's an experiment, no one will come, and we

56

were hoping, by saying the message was secret, that each person would decide for him- or herself whether to come or not."

Josh thought it over. "And you'd show my drawing of an abaguchie to anybody who comes by?"

"Yes. I figured we had to show them *some*thing," said Eddie in a small voice. "We tried to make a picture of it ourselves, but it came out really bad."

"Well, actually, Jake and I haven't come up with an idea for the science fair either, so I guess if I drew the picture, it could be my project too, couldn't it?" said Josh.

Eddie replied agreeably, "Sure! Ask Jake if he wants to help record names and ages and stuff when the kids show up, and he can be in on it too." Anything to keep the boys from telling.

"Okay," said Josh. "We're in. Give me a big sheet of paper, the bigger the better."

Eddie exchanged smiles with Beth and Caroline, then went upstairs and returned with a blank poster board, and Caroline got her set of colored markers with the fine-pointed tips. By the time Josh finished, it was a weird and awful animal that could be found nowhere on earth. It had two tails and silver quills down the ridge of its back. There were scales along its sides, bloody fangs protruding from its horrible mouth, and huge yellow talons on each foot. The eyes were bloodshot, and the ears curved like horns.

Ha! thought Caroline. *They haven't seen anything yet.*

"Would you all like some pop and chips?" came Mrs. Malloy's voice from the kitchen. "We won't be eating for another hour or so. Josh, would you like to stay for dinner?"

"No, thanks. I've got to go pretty soon," he said. "I'll just take a pop."

Eddie quickly smuggled the drawing up to her room, and Caroline collected the colored markers. They sat around the dining room table eating chips, talking about school and snow, which teachers were the best, which were worst, and which hills around Buckman were best for sledding.

Finally Josh said he'd better be going.

"You won't tell any of your friends what we're doing?" Eddie asked.

"Just Jake," Josh promised. "Well, and Wally, maybe. He'd have to know."

Beth said goodbye to him at the door, and when he had gone, she gave Eddie a high five. Eddie, however, looked worried.

"I still wish we hadn't told him," she

said. "Once he tells Jake and Wally that we invited practically everyone, anything could happen. But we didn't have a choice."

"Jake needs a science project as much as you do, remember," Beth said.

"That's true. I just wish I was a partner with anyone but the Hatfords," Eddie said. "They've been bad news ever since we moved to Buckman."

"People can change," said Beth.

"And I'm going to make Wally Hatford fall in love with me," said Caroline.

"Oh, please!" groaned Eddie.

"Did I hear you say you were doing a science project with the Hatfords, Eddie?" Mrs. Malloy called from the other room.

"Yeah, it's sort of a people study, like you suggested," Eddie said. "I'll tell you all about it later."

"So, what do Beth and I do tomorrow?" Caroline asked.

Eddie lowered her voice to a whisper. "Well, Jake and Josh and I have to record the names and ages and grades of each kid, only *I* will be interested in whether they're boys or girls. I don't care about their ages. *I'm* going to prove that more boys show up than girls — that boys are more gullible. But Jake and Josh don't have to know this.

You can line up the kids to go in the garage, Beth, while Caroline takes them in one at a time to show them Josh's picture of the abaguchie."

"Great! The kids will take all their disappointment out on me!" said Caroline.

"Just tell them they participated in a psychological study, and that someday, when I'm a great scientist and I publish the experiment, they'll be famous," Eddie told her.

"I thought you were going to be a doctor of sports medicine or a professional baseball player," said Caroline.

"A doctor-scientist who plays baseball," said Eddie.

Caroline went up to her room and lay down on the bed. Beth and Eddie were getting all the attention these days. Actresses liked to be center stage, and she wanted to get on with her career. She reached under her mattress and pulled out the valentine card she had bought for Wally Hatford. On the envelope she wrote *For My Beloved,* and on the inside she signed the verse *Achingly yours.* And *then,* after she'd admired it for a while, she put her mind on the abaguchie.

Eight

The Experiment

"Because it's stupid, that's why!"

Jake and Josh faced off in their bedroom when Josh came back from the Malloys'. "Experiments are supposed to be about chemicals or electricity and stuff. They're not supposed to be about abaguchies," Jake said.

"It's not about abaguchies, it's about people," Josh told him, sitting down hard on one of the beds. "Eddie's just luring kids over with that note about the abaguchie. She's trying to see which grade is the most gullible."

"I still think it's dumb," said Jake.

"You have a better idea? What project have *we* come up with for the science fair? Nothing. At least we could go in on this with her," Josh argued.

Wally was standing in the shadows outside his brothers' room, listening to the whole thing. He hated it when he was left out of things. "So what's happening?" he asked finally, stepping into the room.

"What do you want, Wally?" Jake snapped, throwing a rolled-up sock at him. "Get out." When Wally got mad, he threw words around. When Jake got mad, he threw socks.

"If it's boys against girls, us against the Malloys, then you've got to let me in on it," Wally said.

"I don't have to do anything but die and pay taxes," Jake said, repeating something he'd heard his dad say once.

"And do a science project," Josh reminded him. "If you're not going to help with the project, I'll take Wally. I said you'd be coming, and we've got it all worked out what each person's going to do."

"Oh, all right," said Jake reluctantly. "But I don't like the way we keep getting tangled up with the girls. I wish the Bensons were back. We always thought up good science projects when they were here."

"What do you mean? We were never in sixth grade until now!" Josh exclaimed. "We never had to do a science experiment before, and you know it."

Jake sighed. "Okay. What do we have to

do at the Malloys'?"

"Well, you and Eddie and I have to record each kid's name, age, and grade, and whether they came because they talked to someone or came on their own. That will figure in the final results."

"Are we going to take Peter?"

"He wanted to see the abaguchie, didn't he?"

"What do *I* get to do?" asked Wally.

"You can help Caroline take the kids into the garage and show them the picture I drew of the abaguchie," said Josh.

"Great!" said Wally. "If any fifth- or sixth-grade guys show up, they'll murder me when all I can show them is a picture!"

"Just tell them they're part of a great experiment," Josh said.

The next afternoon the boys set out for the Malloys', Peter skipping briskly over the planks of the swinging bridge.

"You really want to come, Peter?" Josh asked, knowing that the experiment would be more reliable if every kid came because he wanted to.

"Sure! I want to see the abaguchie!" said Peter.

"You really think the Malloys captured it?" asked Jake.

"Of course! The girls wouldn't lie," said Peter.

Jake gave a low groan.

The sun was bright and warmed the wool stocking caps on their heads as they trudged up the bank to the old Benson house where the Malloys were living.

The girls were briskly setting up two card tables on the back porch. They put a large vat filled with hot cocoa on one; there were three chairs and three notebooks at the other table for the record takers.

"We figured everyone should get a little something, so we're passing out hot chocolate," Beth explained.

"Where's the abaguchie?" asked Peter.

"We'll get to that in a minute," said Eddie. "Come over here, Peter, while we record your name."

Jake and Josh and Eddie sat down at the second card table, and all three recorded Peter's name, his age, and the grade he was in at school.

"Did you show the secret message to anyone, Peter? Or talk to anyone about coming over here?" Eddie asked.

"Only Jake and Josh and Wally," said Peter. He kept looking around. "Is the abaguchie chained up? It won't bite me, will it?"

"It's in the garage, Peter," said Caroline, motioning for him to follow, and she and Wally led Peter to the garage.

This is so dumb, thought Wally as he entered the garage with Caroline. He should have kept his mouth shut and just stayed home. Why was it important for him to do things with Jake and Josh when what they did was really stupid? Going anywhere with Caroline Malloy was double stupid.

Caroline closed the garage door behind them with a creak. Inside, it was dark, and for just a moment Wally could hardly make out what was there. Peter clasped his hand tightly. And then, to his horror, Wally heard Caroline say in a soft little voice, "Wally, you can kiss me if you want to."

"What?" said Wally.

"It's a wonderful place to fall in love," Caroline told him. "So you can kiss me if you want to."

"I don't want to kiss you!" exclaimed Wally. "I don't love you, either. I'm not even sure I *like* you."

"Not even a little?" Caroline asked hopefully. "How do you know you can't fall in love with me if you won't kiss me?"

"But . . . I don't *want* to kiss you. I don't want to fall in love with you, either," Wally told her.

"Oh," said Caroline. "Well, maybe you'll change your mind."

"Sure," said Wally. "When the Mississippi wears rubber pants to keep its bottom dry."

"What?" said Caroline.

Wally just shrugged. It was something he'd heard his mom say once. It was a way of saying *no*. It was a way of saying *never*.

"I want to see the *abaguchie!*" Peter said loudly, tugging at Wally's hand.

Caroline sighed. "Okay, over here," she said, and led Peter to a large box below the loft. It was covered with an old curtain. She pulled back the curtain and shined a flashlight down inside the box. There was the large colored drawing Josh had made of the abaguchie.

Wally stared. It was hideous and spooky. But Peter wasn't impressed.

"Where's the abaguchie?" he asked, his voice growing louder. "The message *said!*"

"It didn't promise the animal was alive, did it?" said Caroline.

Peter was outraged. "You *said!*" he bellowed again.

"What this really is, Peter, is a science experiment," Wally tried to explain. "You're helping Josh and Jake in an experiment they're doing for school."

Peter kicked at the box. "I don't *care!* I don't want to help Josh and Jake. I want to see the abaguchie!"

"Let's go have some cocoa, Peter," said Caroline quickly.

That helped, but only a little. Beth went into the house to find some cookies for him too.

Eddie and Jake exchanged glances. If *Peter*, who was seven, felt cheated, what about the older boys? What if the sixth-graders stood out on the street and told the other kids not to bother? For a while, though, that did not seem to be their problem, for it appeared as though no one else was coming. Three o'clock, three-ten, three-fifteen . . .

"What if nobody comes?" said Eddie worriedly.

"What if this experiment never gets off the ground?" said Jake.

"What if we flunk sixth grade?" said Josh.

And then a couple of third-grade boys started up the driveway, and a girl from Wally's class stood uncertainly out on the road.

"Okay, everybody, get ready," Eddie instructed. "Beth? Wally? Caroline? Where *is* Caroline?"

Nobody seemed to know, but the two third-grade boys were coming up to the porch now, to see the abaguchie, and after Jake and Josh and Eddie had recorded their information and Beth had herded them over to the garage, Wally led them inside without any help.

"It's nothing but a —" Peter said from the steps, a cookie in both fists, but several pairs of hands clapped across his mouth at once.

"So where is it?" one of the third-graders said. "Where's the abaguchie?"

"Over here," said Wally, fumbling his way toward the box in the near darkness, and then he realized he'd forgotten the flashlight. Caroline had it.

At that precise moment, there was a scritching, scratching sound, a huffing, snuffing noise from the loft, and as the three boys lifted their heads, a small light came on above them. There, half hanging from the ladder that led to the loft, was a grotesque creature like no animal they had ever seen. There were horns on its head, claws on its paws, fangs in its mouth, scales on its back, and whether it was covered in feathers or fur, no one could tell, for the creature, moaning and screeching, swung down right over their heads before the light went out. The three boys went tumbling and yelping out of the garage. The fourth-grade girl, who had just given her name and grade to Eddie, didn't even wait to see the abaguchie at all but followed the third-graders as fast as she could back down the driveway.

Jake and Josh and Eddie and Beth stared after them, then at Wally, who collapsed on the back steps, breathing hard.

"What *happened?*" Eddie asked, shaking him by the shoulder. "What *is* it?"

"The . . . the abaguchie!" Wally breathed. Then he added, "I . . . I *think.*"

The twins got up from their chairs and, followed by Beth and Eddie, went slowly, step by step, into the garage. Carefully, Jake opened the door. Inch by inch, they moved inside. Wally stayed a few feet behind them, just in case. Nothing happened. The garage was as dark and still as a cave.

"What are you talking about, Wally?" Jake said, turning around. "There's nothing here that —"

Suddenly the air was split by a half-screech, half-moan; there was a flash of light, and a creature with fangs and claws and scales and feathers swung down over their heads. And then . . . then Caroline dropped the flashlight.

Jake picked it up and shined it on the creature, which was now trying frantically to crawl back up into the little loft where the Malloys stored screens and storm windows.

"Caroline!" they all cried together.

Caroline sat down on the edge of the loft, her feet swinging in the air. "Wasn't I *great?*" she cried. "Wasn't I wonderful?" And while they stared, she climbed back down and stood before them, wearing her mother's fur cap; two Styrofoam cones attached to a headband; plastic vampire fangs in her mouth; and fur mittens with witch's claws glued to the fingers. She also had on an old fur jacket, a feathered boa around her neck and shoulders, and a bath mat, covered with tiny suction cups, thrown over her back.

Eddie started to laugh, then Beth and Josh and Jake. And finally even Wally had to laugh too, even though the joke was on him.

"Caroline, you're just what we need," said Eddie. "Too bad you can't get a grade for this project, too."

"Hey, we've got customers," Josh said, looking out. "Battle stations, everyone."

For the next hour, boys and girls from school came walking up the drive, some alone, some in groups, and every one of them bolted from the garage when Caroline did her act. The older kids hung around a little outside when they made their exit, not quite believing what they'd seen, but Eddie wouldn't let anyone go back a second time, and finally, just after four o'clock, she declared the experiment over.

Jake and Josh finished off the hot chocolate.

"Thirty-two kids showed up!" Eddie said happily, looking over her notebook. "I'd say it was a great success! Eleven were girls and twenty-one were boys. That proves my hypothesis, that boys are more gullible than girls!"

"Hey!" said Jake. "You never said that was what you were after! You said you wanted to see which *grade* was the most gullible."

"So that was *my* little secret." Eddie grinned. "*You* should talk! You didn't have any hypothesis at all."

"I don't care. You should have told us what you were trying to prove before we came over," Jake protested.

But Beth and Josh were already wandering off together, Wally noticed, and they were holding hands!

How could Josh do it? He was only in sixth grade and he was holding a girl's hand. Gross! What kind of a spy was that?

Clutching the picture of the abaguchie in his hand, Peter at his heels, Wally made his way down the hill to the swinging bridge, the sounds of Eddie and Jake's arguing still coming from the porch.

Nine

Big Trouble

The card tables were folded and put away; the urn, emptied of cocoa, was washed and placed back in the cupboard; the paper cups were in the trash; and there was no trace that there had been visitors to the Malloy house that afternoon.

Caroline and her sisters sat sprawled in the living room talking about the experiment.

"That was my finest performance yet!" Caroline bragged, still basking in her glory.

"I'll admit, it was awesome," said Eddie. "No one expected an abaguchie to sail out over their heads, and you didn't have the flashlight on long enough for anybody to be sure of what he'd seen. It's a wonder you didn't break your neck."

"Did you get what you needed for your experiment?" Caroline asked.

"It turned out even better than I

thought," Eddie told her. "About *twice* as many boys than girls turned up. I'm going to get an A on this, you watch. Jake's upset, of course, but at least he got a project out of it."

Beth didn't appear to be even listening, however. She sat with her legs stretched out in front of her, eyes on the ceiling, a grin on her face.

"You're pathetic," Eddie said, looking at her. She reached over with one foot and kicked at Beth's shoe. "Hel . . . lo! Anyone home?" she called.

"Beth, you're a million miles away," Caroline said.

Beth grinned all the more widely. "Josh held my hand," she murmured.

"So?" said Eddie. "He held hands with you in the community play last month, and you didn't look so sappy then. What's the big deal about hands? He probably hasn't washed them in a week. If a guy held hands with me, I'd go take a shower."

"This was spontaneous!" Beth said. "Oh, Eddie, it was so romantic. We were just walking down to the bridge, talking, and our hands accidentally touched and then I felt his fingers lock around mine, and my heart was pounding so hard I felt sure Josh could hear it . . ."

"Spare me," said Eddie, rolling her eyes.

"Well, I'm glad *some*body's lucky in love, because it's not me," Caroline said tragically. From abaguchie to jilted lover, all in one afternoon. "I gave Wally every opportunity to kiss me in the garage and he didn't take it."

Eddie bolted upright on the couch. "Caroline, have you absolutely lost your mind?"

"Why? What's the matter with love?" Caroline answered.

"You're eight years old!" Eddie cried.

"Nine," Caroline corrected her.

"*Just* nine!" said Eddie. "You shouldn't even be *thinking* about kissing and stuff."

"Even *I* haven't been kissed yet," said Beth.

Caroline didn't answer. She had one more thing to try: the beautiful valentine she had bought for Wally. She didn't know how any boy could refuse to fall in love with her after he got such a gorgeous card.

Mr. and Mrs. Malloy came in about six-thirty with a sack of Kentucky Fried Chicken.

"We're going to splurge tonight," said Mrs. Malloy. "It's been a long day, and I'm too tired to cook."

"Fine with us!" said Eddie brightly. "You can bring home KFC any night you want, Mom."

Caroline quickly set the table with paper plates so that there wouldn't be dishes to wash, and soon the family was gathered about the table listening to Mrs. Malloy's account of the conference they had attended at West Virginia University in Morgantown.

They had taken only a few bites of their crispy fried chicken when there was the sound of a car pulling up in the driveway, and a minute later, a knock at the back door.

"Can't we ever have a meal without interruption?" Mrs. Malloy said wearily as Coach Malloy wiped his fingers on his napkin and got up to answer.

A policeman and a woman Caroline had never seen before stood on the back step.

"Sorry to interrupt your dinner, Coach, but I wondered if we could talk to your daughters for a moment," the officer said.

Coach Malloy looked startled. "Of course, come in," he said.

"What's happened?" asked Mrs. Malloy.

The officer and the woman came inside. The woman looked as though she'd been crying.

"This is Ann Weymouth. Her eight-year-old daughter, Lorie, is missing. Ann found this slip of paper in their hallway beside Lorie's schoolbooks."

Coach Malloy took his glasses out of his shirt pocket and read the printed note aloud: " 'Private: This is a secret message. If you want to see the abaguchie, come to 611 Island Avenue between 3 and 4 p.m. tomorrow, Saturday. Free. Do not tell anyone about this message or you will not get in.' "

Coach Malloy's ragged eyebrows shot up high on his forehead as he turned to his daughters. "Who wrote this nonsense? Who's been using my computer?" he asked.

"I did, Dad. I wrote that for a science experiment that Jake and Josh and I were doing for school."

"And you gave it to Mrs. Weymouth's daughter?" he asked incredulously.

"We made copies and put one in the coat pocket of everyone from second to sixth grades," said Beth.

"I helped," added Caroline, eager to share the spotlight with her sisters.

"What are you talking about?" asked Mrs. Malloy, standing up and going over to read the note herself. "*What* abaguchie?

Do you mean to tell me that while your father and I were in Morgantown today, you girls were entertaining practically the whole school here at our house?"

"Not exactly," said Beth. "We kept them outside."

"Except when we took them one at a time into the garage to see the abaguchie — which," Caroline added grandly, "was played by Caroline Lenore Malloy."

"And only thirty-two students showed up," said Eddie. "I wanted to prove that boys are more gullible than girls. It was a people study, just as you suggested, Mom. Josh and Jake and I recorded the data."

Mrs. Malloy sank back down on a chair and closed her eyes.

"What we need to know, girls, is whether Lorie came over here, whether she was with anyone, and about what time she left," said the officer.

"I'll get my data sheet," Eddie said quickly, and went up to her room. She was back in a moment with her notebook.

"Yes, I wrote down that she was the twenty-ninth person to come. So I'd guess she was here about . . . oh, four o'clock," Eddie told them.

"Was she alone?" asked the officer.

"I'm not sure because I don't remember

her exactly," said Eddie. "Beth, do you?"

Mrs. Weymouth looked as though she was on the verge of tears. She pulled a photograph of her daughter from her purse and showed it to Beth and Caroline.

"She was short and sort of giggly, with long, straight brown hair," Beth said, nodding.

The policeman looked concerned. "What we want to know is what happened to her after she left here. We've got an eight-year-old girl who hasn't come home on a cold winter afternoon."

Lorie's mother started to cry again.

Mrs. Malloy looked desperately around at her daughters. *"Think!"* she said. "Did the girl come alone? Did she leave alone?" She turned to Eddie and Beth. "I can't *believe* you did this without our permission. Without even *mentioning* it to us!"

"I'm sorry," Eddie said in a voice so soft that it didn't sound like Eddie at all.

"I wouldn't have known where Lorie went at all if I hadn't found this slip of paper beside her books," Mrs. Weymouth said, wiping her eyes. "Her brother, Dave, is out collecting for the Scouts' canned food drive, but he didn't leave any note about Lorie."

"Tom Hatford's a part-time sheriff's

deputy, and I've got him out looking for Dave," the policeman said. "But I need to know more about Lorie's coming here. Was she alone?"

"No, I remember now," said Beth. "She was with another girl, I think. Well, they were talking together in line, anyway. I'm not sure if they came together or left at the same time."

Eddie checked the list again. "Only eleven girls showed up, and I got all their names. The name before Lorie's is Jackie Maynard, and the name after is Sara Hill."

"I think Jackie's in her class. I haven't heard her mention Sara," said Mrs. Weymouth.

"I'd like to use your phone, Coach," the officer said.

"Please," said Coach Malloy, motioning toward the wall phone in the kitchen.

While the officer looked up the Maynards' number, Caroline, Beth, and Eddie sat under the stern scowl of their father. Caroline dreaded the moment the officer and Lorie's mother left, because she knew her dad was ready to explode at her and her sisters.

The pieces of KFC lay uneaten on the table. The biscuits were growing cold.

The officer closed the phone book and

dialed a number. "Busy," he said, and put the phone down.

While everyone waited for the officer to try again, Coach Malloy erupted. "You girls *knew* you shouldn't be trying a stunt like this or you would have told us about it. You deliberately set this up on a day we'd be out of town."

Eddie, on the verge of tears, stammered, "I just thought y-you and Mom wouldn't like it because . . . well, it was sort of a trick. We were making kids think we had a live abaguchie here when we didn't. I didn't think anything could happen to someone just walking over to our house."

"Well, right now we don't know that any harm has come to Lorie. But it *is* winter; it gets dark early, and we're concerned," the officer said.

The minutes ticked on. The officer tried the number again, and again it was busy. Mrs. Weymouth pulled out another tissue and dabbed at her eyes. Caroline thought about the short, straight-haired girl named Lorie walking back down to the swinging bridge after she'd left the Malloys'. She imagined an abaguchie, or whatever the real animal was, lurking in the brush on the other side. Imagined its sharp teeth tugging at her leg as Lorie stepped off the bridge. Caroline felt sick to her stomach. She would never eat Kentucky Fried Chicken again.

And then her mother's voice intruded. "I don't know what to say, girls. All I know is that when we lived in Ohio, you didn't seem to get in half as much trouble as you do here. Jake and Josh, you said, were in on this project too. Now, I'm not saying who is most at fault, but I think it's time you let the Hatford boys go about their business and you go about yours. I want you to be friendly to them at school, but they shouldn't be coming over here anymore, and I don't want you going over there. I just think things will be better all around that way." She studied her daughters in disappointment and slowly shook her head. "The *first* order of business, however, is to find Lorie Weymouth. And we *will* find her, if our family has to walk the streets all night looking for her."

Ten

New Rule

Tom Hatford put down the phone and reached for his coat. As he thrust his arms into the sleeves, he looked at his sons, who were playing a video game in the living room, and called, "You know anything about the Malloy girls trapping the abaguchie over at their place?"

Jake went on moving the joystick, trying to push Josh's car off the screen. "Ha! They couldn't trap an ant if they sat on it. All they had in their garage was Caroline acting crazy and a picture of an abaguchie that Josh drew."

"What for?" his father asked.

"It was just for an experiment Josh and Eddie and I are doing for our science project. To see who's gullible enough to fall for it," Jake said.

"Did you have anything to do with a secret message sent to a third-grader named

Lorie Weymouth, about seeing the abaguchie at the Malloys'?"

"Heck, no. Caroline stuffed those messages in everyone's coat pocket at school before we ever heard of the project," Josh said.

"Well, it turns out that Lorie's missing, and the sheriff wants me to find her brother. He's out collecting canned food for the Boy Scout food drive. Mrs. Weymouth came home and found her daughter missing, and she's pretty worried. We want to talk with the brother."

"Oh, Tom, you're going to miss dinner again. Can I send a sandwich along?" called Mrs. Hatford from the kitchen.

"No, I'll eat when I get back," Mr. Hatford said.

He went outside, and Wally listened to the Jeep driving off.

"What do you think happened to her?" Wally asked his brothers.

"I don't even know Lorie Weymouth," said Jake.

"If she was there, her name should be on our data sheet," said Josh.

Peter was watching Jake's and Josh's cars collide on the screen. "Maybe the abaguchie got her," he suggested.

"Shut up, Peter," said Jake.

Josh, however, put down his joystick and went into the dining room to get his notebook. He went down the list of names he had recorded along with Jake and Eddie. There it was, near the end of the list: *Lorie Weymouth.* He showed it to his brother.

Wally walked over to the living room window and stared out at the river in the dark. There was nothing but blackness at the bottom of the bank, except where the streetlight shone on the water, and that glistened gold and silver. Anybody who had come looking for the abaguchie that afternoon should have been home long before this. Unless, of course, she had slipped off the swinging bridge and disappeared under the water. Or a kidnapper had picked her up. Or the real abaguchie had got her, as Peter had said.

Mrs. Hatford came into the living room, a fork in one hand, a potholder in the other.

"Lorie's mother must be frantic," she said. "What exactly were the Malloy girls doing?"

"They stuffed secret messages in coat pockets to lure kids over there, and then Jake and Josh and Eddie wrote down their names and what grades they were in to see who showed up," Wally explained, because his mother was looking directly at him.

"You mean you boys were there while all this was going on?"

"Well, sure. We were part of the project, weren't we?" said Jake. "But all the kids I know of went home afterward. I didn't see any girl hanging around."

Mrs. Hatford leaned against the doorway. "Why is it that whenever you boys and the Malloy girls get together something happens? I'm sure plenty of things happened when the Bensons were here that I never heard about, but I must say, the things those girls dream up take the cake! I think it would be a good idea if you'd just leave them alone and do your own projects. Stay on this side of the river from now on. Okay?"

"Fine with me!" said Jake, but Josh didn't answer. Peter looked desperately over at Wally after Mrs. Hatford had gone back in the kitchen.

"No more cookies?" he asked.

"No more cookies," Wally answered. What *he* felt was that he didn't know *how* he felt. There were plenty of times in the past six months when he could not have been happier if he had been told he'd never have to deal with Caroline again. But now that Mrs. Hatford had actually told them not to cross the swinging bridge — to hear it suggested that they couldn't treat the girls like *sisters*, with snowball fights and jokes — well, that wasn't exactly what he wanted to hear either.

It was Josh, however, who was upset.

"Next Monday is Valentine's Day," he said. "I've got a box of Whitman's chocolates for Beth, and I'm not about to give them to her at school in front of everybody."

"Tough," said Jake. "We'll help you eat them."

Mrs. Hatford put dinner on the table and called the boys to the kitchen. It was meat loaf and potatoes and green beans, but Wally didn't feel very hungry. He didn't really know Lorie Weymouth, but he knew who she was, what she looked like. It was a strange feeling to think he might be one of the last persons to have seen her alive. At that very moment, in fact, a stranger might be choking her.

"*Ulp*," went Wally as a bite of meat loaf slid down his throat unchewed.

"Maybe we should go help look for Lorie," Josh said as he pushed a slice of meat loaf from one side of his plate to the other.

"You will stay right here in this house

unless your father needs your help," Mrs. Hatford told him. "The sheriff is out looking too, as well as the Buckman police, and as soon as they locate Lorie's brother, perhaps we'll learn something more. Eat your green beans, Peter."

But Peter put his hands behind him and stared down at his plate. "I'll be sad if I can't go to the Malloys' house anymore," he said. Then he added, "Beth makes good cookies."

"Well, I make cookies too sometimes," said his mother, a little peeved. "You boys survived before the Malloys came here and you can get along without them now. The Malloys aren't the only kids in Buckman."

Dinner was over, dessert eaten, and Josh and Jake were doing the dishes when they heard their father's Jeep coming home again. The boys were waiting by the back door when he walked inside, and Mrs. Hatford came out to the kitchen to warm his plate in the microwave.

"Did they find her, Tom?" she asked.

"Safe and sound at a friend's house. Seems Lorie talked a friend into going to the Malloys' with her, and afterward the friend invited her to stay for dinner. She called home and told her brother, and he was supposed to leave a note for their mother but forgot. Everyone's home now and accounted for."

"Thank goodness!" said Mrs. Hatford.

Mr. Hatford took off his coat and sat down as the microwave dinged. "That was some fool idea, though, to invite half the kids in Buckman over to the Malloys' and then tell them to keep it secret. All *kinds* of things can happen to kids when their folks don't know where they are. I wish you boys hadn't got mixed up in that so-called experiment."

"Well, don't worry," Mrs. Hatford said, "because I've told them not to go over there anymore. Every time our kids and the Malloy kids get together, it seems there's trouble. Let the boys stay on this side of the river and the girls on the other, and maybe we'll have some peace and quiet around here."

But on the way upstairs, Josh whispered to Wally, "I'm getting that Valentine's candy over to Beth no matter what."

The following day, Sunday, after church, the Malloy girls stayed on their side of the river and the Hatfords stayed on theirs. It was one of the most boring afternoons Wally could remember, and he realized with a jolt that the reason was because there was no point in wondering what the Malloy girls were up to, because the answer would be "nothing." He consented to play Monopoly with Peter because there was nothing else to do. He even let Peter put a hotel on Park Place.

They were sprawled on the floor of Wally's bedroom, all Wally's money on one side of the board and Peter's on the other, when Josh stopped by.

"Hey, Peter," said Josh. "Tomorrow's Valentine's Day, you know it?"

"Uh-huh," said Peter. "We're having pink-and-red cupcakes at school."

"Good for you," said Josh. "I've got a problem, though. I bought a box of chocolates for Beth, and Mom doesn't want me to go over there. I'll give you a quarter to deliver it for me."

Peter shook his head. "Mom doesn't want *me* over there either."

"But *your* delivering the candy wouldn't be the same thing as *my* delivering it," Josh said. "Mom wouldn't get mad if you just did what I asked you to do."

"She'd get mad no matter who did it," said Peter.

"Tell you what," Josh went on. "All you have to do is take the box over to the Malloys' and leave it on their porch, between the front door and the storm door. You don't even have to ring the bell or anything. Just leave it, okay? And I'll give you a quarter."

"Okay," said Peter.

He went downstairs and put on his coat and cap, pulled a mitten out of each pocket, then took the yellow box with the big red ribbon and looked it over. There was a handmade card in a handmade envelope taped to the box. It had pieces of red and pink and silver tissue paper pasted on it in unusual shapes, Beth's name in gold, and little red sparkles all over the envelope. Peter shook the box. He smelled it.

"Go, Peter!" Josh commanded.

Still studying the box in his hands, Peter slowly went down the front steps and across the road to the swinging bridge.

Eleven

Gift

Beth had baked two chocolate hearts, one for Josh and one for her father. Coach Malloy had eaten his, but Beth was going to wait until after dark, when no one would see her, then leave Josh's heart on his front porch and ring the bell.

"This is *boring!*" Caroline complained to her sisters as the girls sprawled on Eddie's bed, resting their chins on their hands. "If we can't have anything to do with the Hatfords again, we might as well go back to Ohio. I mean, what have we ever found to do in Buckman that's as exciting as hanging out with the boys?"

"That's the problem with us," Eddie told them as they looked out the window toward the Hatfords' house. "There's lots to do in Buckman — we just haven't gotten involved."

"*I've* been involved! I had a part in the

community play!" Caroline said, failing to mention that she was sick the night of the performance. "But I *still* think doing stuff with the Hatfords — doing things *to* the Hatfords — has been the most fun of all."

"So do I," said Beth in a soft voice, a dreamy voice — and, Caroline noticed, a decidedly sad voice. "But there's got to be more than just leaving a chocolate heart on Josh's porch. I'm going to find a way to be with him if I have to run away to do it."

Both Caroline and Eddie turned and stared at Beth.

"You wouldn't!" said Eddie. "Run away from home over a boy? Over a *Hatford?*"

"Over Josh, I would," Beth said determinedly.

"But where would you go?" asked Caroline. Oh, this was wonderful! Beth was actually talking about forsaking her family and home for the boy she loved! How Caroline wished it were *she* who was thinking of running away — *she* who would do something really romantic! She just *had* to make Wally Hatford fall in love with her, if even for five minutes. "Where would you *live?*" she questioned.

Now it was Beth's turn to stare. "Live? Why, right here, of course! I didn't mean I would run away *to* somewhere. I just meant run off for the day to be with Josh for a while."

"Hey!" said Eddie. "Do you see what I see?"

Beth and Caroline looked toward the window again.

"Somebody's coming across the swinging bridge," said Beth. "It looks like . . . like . . ."

"Peter!" said Caroline. "No one in Buckman takes as long to cross that bridge as Peter Hatford."

"Or finds so many excuses to stop." Eddie laughed.

They studied the young boy standing at the cable handrail, watching the water flow under the bridge.

"What's he got under his arm?" mused Beth.

"Looks like a book. A dictionary?" Caroline guessed.

"It's not a dictionary, it's a box," said Eddie, craning her neck and staring hard out the window.

Down below, Peter started forward again. Yes, it *was* a box, Caroline decided. A yellow box. Peter was holding it in both hands now and studying it as he crossed the halfway point on the bridge and kept coming. Now she saw him hold the box up to his ear and shake it.

"You know what I think he's got? A box of Whitman's chocolates," Eddie said, beginning to smile. "Doesn't it look like it's wrapped in cellophane? And isn't that a wide red ribbon across the front?"

"Beth, I'll bet it's for you!" Caroline cried excitedly. "I'll bet Josh sent it over here with Peter."

They watched in fascination as Peter held the box to his face and appeared to be sniffing it. Yes, it *was* a box of Whitman's chocolates. The girls would recognize one of them anywhere. Caroline had seen rows and rows of them in the drugstore.

"They're chocolates, all right," Beth said.

"Or they *were* — what will be left of them if Peter doesn't stop shaking them." Eddie laughed as Peter shook the box still again.

Peter came off the bridge at last, but he took only two steps up the long hill to their house before he stopped, looked over his shoulder, then sat down on a large rock there on the bank.

"*Now* what?" Beth wondered aloud, then gasped as she watched Peter pull off the ribbon and work his finger under the cellophane in one corner.

"He's *opening* it!" Caroline shrieked.

95

"He's going to eat your candy, Beth!"

"I don't believe this," murmured Eddie.

"*I* believe it!" said Caroline.

Peter was holding his mitten in his mouth while his finger probed around under the cellophane, trying to lift a corner of the lid. But it didn't seem to be working, and so, with a shrug, Peter dropped both his mittens on the ground and gently tore all the cellophane off the yellow box. The girls stared in fascination.

They watched as Peter opened the lid. They saw him study the diagram on the inside. They saw him lift up the cardboard over the first layer of chocolates to peer at the candy beneath. And finally his hand roamed around the top, started to descend over a chocolate, paused, then plucked a piece out of the box and popped it into his mouth.

"My candy!" Beth wailed, laughing nonetheless.

"At least, we *think* it's your candy," said Caroline. Who was to say it might not be for *her?* — a box of Whitman's chocolates from Wally?

Peter seemed to be having a marvelous time. He probably had selected a nougat, Caroline decided, since those were usually the largest pieces of all and his jaws were still moving up and down.

"You'd better get up here, Peter." Eddie laughed. "If Josh sees what you're doing, you're dead, kid."

Any minute now, the girls expected Peter to close the lid of the box. Any minute they expected to see him get to his feet and bring the candy on up to the house.

To their surprise, however, Peter pondered the diagram under the lid again, and once more his hand hovered over the layer of chocolates.

"*Look* at him!" cried Eddie.

Peter picked up another chocolate, looked it over, then put it back in the box and traded it for something else.

"Oh, gross!" cried Caroline.

The second chocolate went into his mouth.

"If you're lucky, Beth, you may get a piece or two before they're gone," Eddie told her.

It appeared as though Peter had barely swallowed the second piece before he selected a third, and then, to their horror, the Malloy girls watched as he poked his finger first in one chocolate, shook his head, then another, shook his head, and finally, finding a candy to his liking, popped it into his mouth and sat tapping both feet on the ground.

But it was when he began nibbling a corner off first one piece of candy, then another, that Eddie said, "Somebody ought to go out there and stop him."

"Maybe it's his own candy," said Caroline. "Maybe somebody gave him a box and he's just sitting out there enjoying it."

"On *our* side of the river?" said Eddie. "Come on. Put on your jackets and let's go pretend we're just out walking."

The girls clattered downstairs, took their jackets off the pegs by the back door, and headed down the hill toward the swinging bridge.

Peter was holding a large chocolate out in front of him, examining it from all sides, when the Malloy girls suddenly appeared in front of him.

Caroline saw him freeze. The chocolate dropped from his fingers back into the box and he sat like a statue on the rock. A thin trickle of marshmallow creme oozed out one side of his mouth.

"Hi, Peter," Beth called. "Looks like you're having a picnic."

"All by yourself," added Caroline.

"It looks to me like you're celebrating Valentine's Day a day early," said Eddie.

Without taking his eyes off the girls, Peter scrunched up the cellophane. His fingers raked up all the empty paper cups and he thrust them under him, there on the rock.

The girls took a step closer. The marshmallow creme slid down Peter's chin and onto his jacket.

"Yum! Whitman's chocolates!" said Eddie. "Who gave you the candy, Peter? Your girlfriend?"

Peter swallowed and thrust the box toward Beth, and as soon as it was safely in her hands, he leaped off the rock and went racing back across the swinging bridge.

The girls looked down at the box, then at the cellophane on the ground. There was a card taped to the cellophane. On it someone had drawn a beautiful heart, decorated with little pieces of pink and red tissue paper and covered with red sparkles. In the middle were the initials *J* + *B*.

Twelve

Like Two Hot Coals

"So how long does it take to drop a box of chocolates on a porch?" Josh murmured to Wally as they sat in front of the TV.

"Not this long," Wally said. "We saw him cross the bridge, though. We know where he was headed, right?"

"You don't suppose Caroline got to him first and took the chocolates herself, do you?" Josh asked warily.

Wally shrugged. "Anything is possible with Caroline."

They looked up to see Jake observing them from the doorway. "So, what are you guys doing?" he asked. "What's up?"

"What do you mean?" said Josh. "We're watching TV."

"With the Mute button on? What's happening, anyway?"

"Waiting for Peter, that's all," Josh said. "I sent him on a little errand."

Jake came over and sat down. "Waiting for Peter to do what?" And when he got no answer, he grinned. "Waiting for Peter to deliver a valentine, maybe? You might as well tell me, because I'll find out somehow."

"Waiting for Peter to deliver a two-pound box of Whitman's chocolates to Beth Malloy," said Wally, answering for Josh.

Jake stared at his twin. "Are you crazy? After all we've done to drive the Malloys out of Buckman, you're giving Beth a valentine? *Chocolates?* Do you want them to stay here forever?"

"I wouldn't mind," said Josh truthfully.

Jake clutched at his head. "What's *happening* to us? We're all going soft, that's what! Beth's your *girl*friend, Josh! Who are you kidding?"

"She is *not!*" said Josh. "You wanted me to spy, didn't you? I can't very well spy if they won't have anything to do with us. If Valentine's Day comes and goes and Beth doesn't get a present from me, do you think she'll tell me anything anymore?"

"Yeah? So what's she told you so far that we didn't know already?" said Jake. "I'll bet she's given *you* a valentine too, hasn't she? Baked some fancy cookies or something?"

"No, she hasn't, but if she does, I'll just throw them out," Josh said.

There were footsteps on the porch, and the front door opened a crack. Wally and his brothers stopped talking and watched as the door opened wider still and Peter slid noiselessly inside. He was tiptoeing across the hall, trying to get upstairs without being seen.

"Peter?" said Josh.

Peter stopped with one foot in the air.

Josh got up from the sofa and went out into the hall, Wally and Jake at his heels. Peter put his foot on the stairs and paused again, avoiding Josh's eyes.

"Don't you want your quarter?" Josh asked, digging in his pocket.

"No, you can keep it," Peter murmured, and took another step.

"Why? You delivered the candy, didn't you?"

Peter didn't answer.

"Peter! What *happened?*" Josh asked. "You didn't drop it in the river, did you?"

Peter shook his head.

"What *did* you do?" Josh asked in alarm.

"I gave it to Beth," said Peter. "She came along and I just gave it to her."

Josh looked relieved. "Well, what did she say?"

think I'm nuts, sending her a box of
eaten chocolates."

hy don't you just call her up?" Wally
sted.

om would hear, and anyway, I'd
leave a note. You come with me,
me up on their back-porch roof, and
p it in Beth's window."

right, but all we need is for the
ys to call the police and report a bur-
n the roof, and Mom would *really*
ut."

n't tell Jake, though. You know how
Josh cautioned him.

, however, followed Josh around like
ow, and when he saw him leaving the
with Wally, he came too.

o asked you?" said Josh.

, whatever you're going to do, I can
aid Jake.

? Well, I just want to tell Beth that
e those chocolates. I don't want her
I did. I've written her a note, and
guys will boost me up onto the
oof, I'll just slip the note in her
, see what the girls are up to."

You'd better explain why you sent
tead of taking them over yourself,"
him.

use Mom doesn't want us to have

Peter shrugged. "I don't know."

Josh reached out and turned Peter around. "What's that on your jacket?" His voice rose. "What's that on your *chin?* Peter, you ate those chocolates, didn't you!"

Peter broke away and dashed upstairs, his brothers after him, and managed to lock his door before Josh could get it open.

Josh put his mouth to the door. "Boy, you'd better not come out of there as long as you live," he whispered through the crack. "You'd better not come out of there until I go to college, Peter, because I'm going to pulverize you."

There was a small squeak from behind the door. "I didn't eat them all!" Peter said.

Josh banged his head against the door.

"How many *did* you eat?" asked Wally.

There was a pause, but the boys could hear Peter counting. "Maybe four," he said. "I only took a little bite off the others."

Josh moaned.

"Why?" asked Wally. "Why would you open the chocolates Josh was sending to Beth?"

"I was hungry!" Peter answered in a pitiful little voice.

"See what a dumb idea that was, Josh? See what trouble a girlfriend is?" said Jake.

Mrs. Hatford came upstairs. "What's going on?" she asked. "Where's Peter?"

"In his room," said Wally.

"What's he doing in there? Why are you three standing out here?"

"We're trying not to kill him," said Josh, and went into the bedroom he shared with Jake, shutting the door behind him.

Mrs. Hatford looked at Jake and then at Wally and then at the two closed doors. "No," she said finally. "This is too nice a day to ruin. I don't think I want to know." And she went back downstairs.

Peter stayed in his room most of the day, and Josh was too angry to come out of his. Just before dinner, however, when dark had settled in, the doorbell rang, and when Wally answered it, all he found was a box. A low square box with the words *For Josh* on the outside. He took it upstairs, where the twins were playing a computer game.

"What's that?" asked Josh.

"Somebody rang the doorbell, and when I answered, I found this," Wally said.

"So open it!" said Jake. "Looks like my hunch was right."

Josh opened the box. Instead of fancy cookies, there was a large, delicious-

looking chocolate heart, wit[...] in frosting.

"See? See?" said Jake. "[...] friend."

Josh's face and neck were[...] didn't say a word as the [...] examining the chocolate[...] sniffed it and turned it fr[...] To Wally, it smelled simply[...]

"Okay, so let's see yo[...] That's what you said you'[...] his twin.

Josh hesitated.

"You aren't even going [...] Wally.

"Go ahead! Taste it [...] waiting," said Jake. "If Be[...] friend, I dare you to thro[...]

Josh swallowed. "Of co[...] girlfriend," he said quick[...] bet it's made out of som[...] took one last look at the[...] then opened the window[...] over the porch roof and[...] below.

After dinner, with P[...] away from Josh as he c[...] took Wally aside and s[...] over to Beth's and lea[...]

anything more to do with the Malloys," Josh said.

"Sure. So you send Peter. Now, that makes sense," Jake jeered.

Josh shrugged. "All right, so I don't know what to say to a girl when I give her candy. So what? You wouldn't know what to say either. If I'm going to spy on her, I have to pretend to like her."

They crossed the bridge in the February darkness, the twins in front, Wally walking behind. He didn't know why he was even along, to tell the truth. Jake *would* have to horn in just when Josh and Wally were beginning to do things together, when Josh was beginning to confide in him. Wally could see it all now. No matter how good a friend he was to Josh, Jake and Josh would always be best friends because they were twins, and he'd be stuck with Peter.

They reached the other side of the bridge and started up the hill toward the Malloys' back door. Wally tried to remember what things had been like when the Bensons lived in the house. Weird, but he was having a hard time remembering exactly what things they used to do with the Benson boys that were so much fun. He must have crossed the swinging bridge and come up the hill to the Bensons' house dozens and dozens of times — hundreds, even — but what did they *do* when they got together? Played baseball, maybe. Played Clue. Flew model planes. Played Kick the Can. It was all fun stuff, but somehow it didn't seem as exciting as it once had.

As the boys reached the top of the hill, they could see a square yellow patch of light from the kitchen window shining on the hard ground. The porch light was off, however.

Josh dug one hand into his pocket for the note he had written to Beth.

"I just want you to boost me up on the porch roof, and I'll slide this note under her window."

"What if the window won't open?" asked Jake.

"I already thought of that. I'll just tape it to the glass," said Josh, and showed them a roll of tape in his pocket.

Wally began to feel useless. "So what am I, your cheering section?" he asked. "I don't think you need me at all. I think —"

He didn't finish. He stopped in mid-sentence and didn't even close his mouth. Because there, just beyond the garage, were two shining eyes, glowing like hot coals in the darkness.

Wally could only gasp and clutch his

Peter shrugged. "I don't know."

Josh reached out and turned Peter around. "What's that on your jacket?" His voice rose. "What's that on your *chin?* Peter, you ate those chocolates, didn't you!"

Peter broke away and dashed upstairs, his brothers after him, and managed to lock his door before Josh could get it open.

Josh put his mouth to the door. "Boy, you'd better not come out of there as long as you live," he whispered through the crack. "You'd better not come out of there until I go to college, Peter, because I'm going to pulverize you."

There was a small squeak from behind the door. "I didn't eat them all!" Peter said.

Josh banged his head against the door.

"How many *did* you eat?" asked Wally.

There was a pause, but the boys could hear Peter counting. "Maybe four," he said. "I only took a little bite off the others."

Josh moaned.

"*Why?*" asked Wally. "Why would you open the chocolates Josh was sending to Beth?"

"I was hungry!" Peter answered in a pitiful little voice.

"See what a dumb idea that was, Josh? See what trouble a girlfriend is?" said Jake.

Mrs. Hatford came upstairs. "What's going on?" she asked. "Where's Peter?"

"In his room," said Wally.

"What's he doing in there? Why are you three standing out here?"

"We're trying not to kill him," said Josh, and went into the bedroom he shared with Jake, shutting the door behind him.

Mrs. Hatford looked at Jake and then at Wally and then at the two closed doors. "No," she said finally. "This is too nice a day to ruin. I don't think I want to know." And she went back downstairs.

Peter stayed in his room most of the day, and Josh was too angry to come out of his. Just before dinner, however, when dark had settled in, the doorbell rang, and when Wally answered it, all he found was a box. A low square box with the words *For Josh* on the outside. He took it upstairs, where the twins were playing a computer game.

"What's that?" asked Josh.

"Somebody rang the doorbell, and when I answered, I found this," Wally said.

"So open it!" said Jake. "Looks like my hunch was right."

Josh opened the box. Instead of fancy cookies, there was a large, delicious-looking chocolate heart, with $B + J$ written in frosting.

"See? See?" said Jake. "She's your girl-friend."

Josh's face and neck were bright red. He didn't say a word as the boys took turns examining the chocolate heart. They sniffed it and turned it from side to side. To Wally, it smelled simply delicious.

"Okay, so let's see you throw it out. That's what you said you'd do," Jake told his twin.

Josh hesitated.

"You aren't even going to *taste* it?" cried Wally.

"Go ahead! Taste it or toss it; we're waiting," said Jake. "If Beth's not your girl-friend, I dare you to throw it out."

Josh swallowed. "Of course she's not my girlfriend," he said quickly. "And you can bet it's made out of something gross." He took one last look at the chocolate heart, then opened the window and tossed it out over the porch roof and onto the ground below.

After dinner, with Peter sitting as far away from Josh as he could manage, Josh took Wally aside and said, "I have to go over to Beth's and leave her a note. She must think I'm nuts, sending her a box of half-eaten chocolates."

"Why don't you just call her up?" Wally suggested.

"Mom would hear, and anyway, I'd rather leave a note. You come with me, boost me up on their back-porch roof, and I'll slip it in Beth's window."

"All right, but all we need is for the Malloys to call the police and report a burglar on the roof, and Mom would *really* freak out."

"Don't tell Jake, though. You know how he is," Josh cautioned him.

Jake, however, followed Josh around like a shadow, and when he saw him leaving the house with Wally, he came too.

"Who asked you?" said Josh.

"Hey, whatever you're going to do, I can help," said Jake.

"Yeah? Well, I just want to tell Beth that Peter ate those chocolates. I don't want her to think *I* did. I've written her a note, and if you guys will boost me up onto the porch roof, I'll just slip the note in her window, see what the girls are up to."

"Ha! You'd better explain why you sent Peter instead of taking them over yourself," Jake told him.

"Because Mom doesn't want us to have

anything more to do with the Malloys," Josh said.

"Sure. So you send Peter. Now, that makes sense," Jake jeered.

Josh shrugged. "All right, so I don't know what to say to a girl when I give her candy. So what? You wouldn't know what to say either. If I'm going to spy on her, I have to pretend to like her."

They crossed the bridge in the February darkness, the twins in front, Wally walking behind. He didn't know why he was even along, to tell the truth. Jake *would* have to horn in just when Josh and Wally were beginning to do things together, when Josh was beginning to confide in him. Wally could see it all now. No matter how good a friend he was to Josh, Jake and Josh would always be best friends because they were twins, and he'd be stuck with Peter.

They reached the other side of the bridge and started up the hill toward the Malloys' back door. Wally tried to remember what things had been like when the Bensons lived in the house. Weird, but he was having a hard time remembering exactly what things they used to do with the Benson boys that were so much fun. He must have crossed the swinging bridge and come up the hill to the Bensons' house dozens and dozens of times — hundreds, even — but what did they *do* when they got together? Played baseball, maybe. Played Clue. Flew model planes. Played Kick the Can. It was all fun stuff, but somehow it didn't seem as exciting as it once had.

As the boys reached the top of the hill, they could see a square yellow patch of light from the kitchen window shining on the hard ground. The porch light was off, however.

Josh dug one hand into his pocket for the note he had written to Beth.

"I just want you to boost me up on the porch roof, and I'll slide this note under her window."

"What if the window won't open?" asked Jake.

"I already thought of that. I'll just tape it to the glass," said Josh, and showed them a roll of tape in his pocket.

Wally began to feel useless. "So what am I, your cheering section?" he asked. "I don't think you need me at all. I think —"

He didn't finish. He stopped in mid-sentence and didn't even close his mouth. Because there, just beyond the garage, were two shining eyes, glowing like hot coals in the darkness.

Wally could only gasp and clutch his

brothers' sleeves, but Jake and Josh had seen the eyes too, and neither of them moved a muscle. They didn't even seem to be breathing.

For what seemed like sixty seconds the boys stood frozen, the two hot coals staring back at them.

Then the creature took a step forward.

"Abaguchie!" Wally croaked, and suddenly the three boys were stumbling onto the Malloys' back porch, pounding on the door, so that when it opened at last, they tumbled inside and fell at the feet of Coach Malloy.

Thirteen

The Confrontation

"Boys?" said Caroline's father, as though he wasn't sure whether the creatures sprawled at his feet were animal or vegetable.

"We saw it!" Jake gasped.

"The abaguchie!" said Wally.

By now the girls had gathered, wide-eyed, in the kitchen, and Mrs. Malloy came up from the basement where she had been doing the laundry. The whole family was staring at the Hatford boys, who were awkwardly getting to their feet.

"You saw something outside just now?" Coach Malloy quizzed them.

"Standing right beside the garage! It was horrible!" said Wally.

"Fiery red eyes!" said Josh.

"Pointed ears!" said Jake.

"A long pointed tail. Sort of like a . . . a devil's tail," Josh finished uncertainly.

And when Coach Malloy folded his arms

across his chest and raised one eyebrow, Wally added, "It was coming right at us."

Mr. and Mrs. Malloy exchanged glances.

"What were you guys doing over here in the first place?" the girls' father asked.

"We were just out walking," Jake insisted.

"Along the river," said Josh.

"And we weren't doing *any*thing!" said Wally.

Coach Malloy took a flashlight and went out in the backyard to look around. But Mrs. Malloy said, "You were walking along the river way up here in our yard?"

At that Josh blushed, and when that happened, Beth's face grew pink as well. A minute went by in silence. Then another. Finally the girls' father came back inside.

"Didn't see a thing," he said. He put one hand on Josh's shoulder and sat down on the edge of the table. "Listen, you guys," he said. "Let me tell you something. I think it's time you made other friends and started hanging out with other boys. Leave the girls alone."

"Daddy!" Beth protested, humiliated that he would say such a thing, but Coach Malloy held up one hand to stop her.

"I don't know how it happens," he went on. "I'm not even sure exactly *what* happens, for that matter. But whenever the seven of you get together, the roof falls in, so to speak. Surely you boys had other friends before my daughters came to Buckman."

The girls were aghast. They had never heard their father talk like this. It seemed so *rude*. Caroline couldn't stand it. If her father actually forbade the Hatford boys to come over, what in the world would she do for fun? Where would she ever find the same excitement, the romance, the mystery, the *revenge?*

But Wally was talking next. "We *did* have best friends, but they moved out when you moved in," he explained.

"There are other boys in this town, surely!" said Mrs. Malloy. "You don't have to spend all your time over here."

Caroline burst into tears. "I can't believe what you're *saying!* How can you be so rude? You're telling the Hatfords they can't cross the river in their very own town?"

"Now, wait a minute —" said the coach.

But Eddie interrupted. "It's still a free country."

"We don't tell *you* when *your* friends can come over," cried Beth, real tears in her eyes, while the Hatford boys stared, openmouthed. She turned to her mother. "We don't stop *you* from being friends with that awful woman in the Faculty

112

Wives' Club who —"

"Now, girls!" said their father.

Suddenly Josh reached out, handed Beth his note, then charged toward the door and out into the night, his brothers at his heels.

Beth stared at the folded piece of paper for a moment, then ran up to her room and slammed her door.

"Well, Jean, it looks like we blew it," said the coach.

"You'd make a fine dictator!" said Eddie, and followed her sister upstairs.

As her parents stared helplessly after Eddie, Caroline grandly walked over to the staircase, put one foot on the bottom step, and said, "You may win this battle, General, but don't be surprised if you lose the war." And with her head held high, she too went upstairs.

As soon as she reached Beth's room, Caroline slipped inside and crawled onto the bed beside Beth and Eddie. Beth, her cheeks pink, had opened the note, and she handed it to her sisters. It was Josh's handwriting, all right:

I shouldn't have sent Peter with the chocolates.
I didn't know he'd eat them.
XXXOOO Josh

Caroline looked at the note, then at Beth, whose eyes were wide with delight. Josh was sending hugs and kisses? This was even more romantic than the box of chocolates. This was *almost* like kissing Beth in person. Beth Malloy had *almost* been kissed.

"I sure don't want any boy sending *me* X's and O's" said Eddie disapprovingly.

"Why?" asked Beth. "Don't you ever want to fall in love?"

"Sure," said Eddie, "but I don't want a boy acting romantic now. I want the boys on the baseball team to look at me and see a *pitcher*, not a girlfriend."

Caroline could hardly stand it. She was caught up in romance. Going into her own room, she took out the valentine she had bought for Wally Hatford, the one that said *For My Beloved* on the envelope, and on the inside, where she had signed it *Achingly yours*, she added a row of X's and a row of O's.

Fourteen

Party

When Wally and his brothers got home, they were met at the door by Peter.

"I've got a *surprise!*" he said, eager to make friends with Josh again, and led them up to his room.

"Boy, Peter, this better be good," Josh muttered.

Peter closed the door after him, then reached under his bed and pulled out a low square box. Inside the box were the crumpled remains of a chocolate heart.

"Look what I found outside! Somebody threw it away, and it's delicious!" he said, smacking his lips. He pushed the box toward Josh. "I'm sorry I ate Beth's chocolates, but I saved half of this for you."

Wally stared. Josh stared. Jake put out one finger and dug into the center of the chocolate heart. He licked his finger.

"So you bet it was gross, huh?" he said

to Josh. "So Beth's not your girlfriend and you only hang around her to spy? If you're a spy, then I'm the president." He went across the hall to the boys' room and shut the door.

Josh looked at Peter. "How did you find this box?"

"I wondered where you guys had gone, and when I went outside with my flashlight to see if you were there, I found the box." He looked from Wally to Josh and back again. "What'd I *do?*" he asked. "What's wrong?"

"You're still breathing, that's what," said Josh.

Wally wrote a letter to Bill Benson in Georgia:

Dear Bill (and Danny and Steve and Tony and Doug),

I don't know what's happening here, but things were never like this before you guys moved away.

I don't know if the Whomper, the Weirdo, and the Crazie are friends or enemies.

I don't know if they're nuts or not.

I don't even know how we feel about them anymore. Josh is in love with Beth, I think, and Caroline is acting strange. We're not supposed to cross the river, and nobody ever told us before where we could and couldn't go in this town.

By the time you guys get back here, if you ever do, Josh and Beth will probably be married, and Jake and I will have joined the marines. I will probably have to run off to get away from Caroline, but then she'd only go after Peter instead.

COME BACK! NOW!!!!!
                                                    Wally

On Monday, Valentine's Day, Wally took an old shoe box without any decorations whatsoever on it, and with a Magic Marker, simply wrote his name on the side of the box. He cut a slit in the top for valentines. He wished he were in sixth grade and didn't have to go to any stupid Valentine's party. He would much rather have a Halloween party, where everyone got to roam around the room in masks and gulp handfuls of candy corn.

When he got to school, he walked into the classroom to find Caroline Malloy sitting primly in her seat, wearing a red velvet dress with a white lace collar, and smiling a smile as wide as a banana.

"*Hello,* Wally," she purred as he took his seat, and she leaned forward so far that he could feel her breath on his neck.

"Hi," said Wally without turning around, and leaned forward so that she couldn't possibly touch him. Caroline Malloy as herself was bad enough, but Caroline in a red velvet dress meant trouble.

"Happy Valentine's Day," came the voice behind him again.

Wally got up and crossed the room to sharpen his pencil and stayed there until Miss Applebaum took the roll. When he finally sat down again, he realized that Caroline was using the edge of her ruler to trace a large heart on the back of his shirt.

All day Wally did his best not even to look at Caroline Malloy. He tried his best not to listen to her. He wished it were three o'clock and he could go home, but there had to be a party, and at two o'clock, Miss Applebaum said to put their books away and go collect the valentine shoe boxes from the windowsill, where friends had been slipping valentines all day.

Then the teacher sent a boy around with a tray of paper cups filled with pink punch,

and a girl followed carrying a tray of cupcakes with red-and-white frosting, and
somebody else passed out little paper cups
filled with heart-shaped candies that said
things like HEY KID and HOT MAMA, BLUE
EYES and I DIG U.

Wally took a bite of his cupcake with the
red-and-white icing and opened the lid of
his shoe box. There were just a handful of
valentines, the silly kind, from his buddies,
and that was just fine with Wally. He didn't
want any dumb valentines from girls that
would make Jake tease him.

He had just taken another bite of his
cupcake when something flew over his left
shoulder and landed on his desk. Wally
picked up an orange candy heart and
looked at it.

NEW LOVE, it said on the heart.

Wally popped it in his mouth and stared
straight ahead.

Ping!

Another candy came flying over his right
shoulder and hit his hand. Wally didn't
move, but the candy was resting against his
thumb, so he finally reached over with his
other hand and picked it up.

SWEET DREAMS, it said.

Wally popped that in his mouth too.

This time Wally felt fingers on the back

of his neck and a candy tucked under his collar.

Wally grabbed at the candy and tossed it behind him, but it came flying back again, and he could not help noticing that the writing said SWEETHEART. Wally's ears turned as red as the frosting on his cup-cake.

The class played a few word games next. Miss Applebaum wrote *Valentine* on the blackboard, and the class was supposed to see who could make the most words out of the letters by mixing them up. They sang songs and did relay races with shiny red apples. Wally stayed as far away from Caroline as he could.

When the bell rang at three, Wally was the first one out of his seat. He threw his cupcake wrapper and paper cup in the trash and hurried out to the coatrack. He tossed on his jacket and had just turned to leave when he found himself face-to-face with Caroline in her red velvet dress with the lace collar.

"For you," she said sweetly, pressing an envelope into his hand.

Wally stared at Caroline, at the weird smile on her face. Then he looked down at the envelope.

For My Beloved, it said.

Wally raced outside as though bees were after him, afraid lest anyone else should see the words, and thrust the card at the first person he met, who happened to be Jake.

"For you," he said.

Fifteen

Love Lost

What Caroline couldn't stand was that all the excitement in the family these days — among the three girls, anyway — seemed to be happening to Beth, not to her.

Beth was absolutely impossible. Since Josh had sent her chocolates and then a note with *X*'s and *O*'s, Beth was dreamy and giggly and excited and silly and didn't even know what day it was half the time. She put a white sock on one foot and a pink one on the other and didn't even notice.

This should all be happening to me, Caroline thought, *not Beth.* Yet for a week after Valentine's Day, Wally wouldn't even speak to her. He wouldn't even *look* at her. How could anybody with half a brain resist a girl in a red velvet dress with a white lace collar? How could he not even *thank* her for a card addressed *For My Beloved* and signed *Achingly yours?*

Wally was mad at Caroline, and Jake and Josh were mad at Eddie about the science project. They had not gotten a very good grade on it. In fact, at the science fair, the teacher had used it as an example of how a project should *not* be done. First, she'd written, the three students had not started out with the same hypothesis, that boys were more gullible than girls; second, there was no sure way of knowing whether students had come because they really believed they would see the abaguchie or just for fun; third . . .

Eddie had been too discouraged to read the rest of her teacher's comments. She had crumpled up the paper her teacher had returned and left it on the kitchen table for her parents to read, but not before Caroline had seen a big red C− at the top. The only people who seemed to be getting along these days were Beth and Josh.

At lunchtime in the all-purpose room one day, Caroline was eating with some of her friends, and one of the fourth-grade girls was talking about *her* boyfriend. Caroline stared at her in dismay. A fourth-grade girl actually *did* have a boyfriend? And Caroline didn't?

"The problem is," the girl was saying importantly, "boys are shy. A boy can be in love and not even know it. And if he *does* know it, he won't admit it."

"Really?" said Caroline.

"Really," said her friend. "If you see a boy looking at you sideways out of the corner of his eye, it means he likes you. But he'll never tell you so, and when he's around his friends, he might even insult you so no one will guess how he really feels."

That's it! thought Caroline. *Wally's just shy.*

The first thing to do was to see whether or not he was watching her out of the corner of his eye. So after lunch, when the whole class was making maps for social studies, Caroline went to the pencil sharpener to sharpen all her colored pencils, whether they needed it or not. She put the green pencil in the sharpener and began to turn the handle. Then suddenly she whirled around and stared straight at Wally Hatford.

She couldn't tell if he had been watching her or not, but he was certainly watching her now. In fact, when he saw Caroline staring straight at him, his own pencil fell out of his hand and onto the floor.

Aha! thought Caroline. She turned back to the sharpener again and did her blue pencil, then the red, and when she was halfway through sharpening the purple one, she whirled again, her eyes on Wally, and he seemed to rise two inches off his chair.

So he *was* watching her, she decided. And with a knowing smile on her face, she collected her colored pencils, went back to her desk, and tickled Wally lightly behind his ear with the tip of the blue pencil. He swatted it away as though it were a mosquito.

"That's okay, Wally," she whispered, leaning forward so that she was breathing on his neck again. "I know you really like me."

"I do not!" Wally said aloud, and the whole class looked up. So did the teacher.

"Yes, Wally?" she said.

"I *don't!*" said Wally, his ears as red as his sweater.

"You don't what?"

"Really like Caroline," said Wally, and now the red was spreading to his face and neck.

Miss Applebaum looked puzzled. "Did someone say you did?"

"Caroline did, and I *don't!*" Wally's

words shot from his mouth like bullets.

Caroline was surprised to find that her own cheeks and ears seemed to be getting feverish, and when the other kids giggled, her skin grew warmer still.

"Caroline, perhaps you could save your personal conversation with Wally till after school," the teacher said.

"No!" said Wally again. "Not then, not ever!"

"Oh," said the teacher. "Well, if you have anything to say to Wally, Caroline, please write him a note and give it to him after class."

"*No!*" Wally yelped again. "She already did, and I *don't* really like her."

Caroline had never heard Wally talk up like this in class. Usually he was on the quiet side, rather dreamy and somewhat polite — to the teacher, anyway. But now his voice was too loud, his face too red, and it could mean only one thing: that he really, *really* liked her, because he had to try so hard to convince everyone that he didn't. She smiled to herself and leaned over her map again, exchanging winks with the friend she'd talked to at lunch.

After school, the Hatford boys were far down the sidewalk before Caroline and her sisters came out. Caroline hadn't told Beth and Eddie about the valentine she'd given Wally because she knew Beth thought *she* was the only one who could be in love, and Eddie would call her ridiculous. So she couldn't very well tell them what Wally had said in class. Thoughtfully, she followed along behind her sisters while they talked of school and this and that, and wondered how in the world to make a boy fall in love with her just long enough for her to experience romance.

When they came to the swinging bridge, however, Eddie went first, and Beth hung back, so Caroline stepped onto the bridge. When she had taken only a few steps, she glanced over her shoulder in time to see Beth taping a small piece of paper to the cable handrail.

Caroline quickly faced forward again as Beth came up behind her.

A note! Beth was taping a secret message to Josh, Caroline was sure of it. This was wonderful! It was wonderful because it was full of mystery and romance and intrigue. And it was awful because it was happening to Beth instead of her.

The girls gathered in the kitchen for corn chips and pop. Mrs. Malloy was ironing shirts in the dining room and listening to a symphony on a CD. Caroline and her sisters talked for a few minutes, and then Beth and Eddie took their books upstairs. As soon as Beth was out of the kitchen, Caroline put on her coat again and slipped out the back door. Darting from bush to bush, she made her way down the hill until she found a spot where she was sure she could not be seen from either Beth's window or the other side of the bridge. Then she waited.

She didn't have to wait long. Almost no time at all, in fact, because thirty seconds later, she saw Josh Hatford saunter down the bank, hands in his pockets. Glancing quickly over his shoulder, he stopped on the bridge, resting his arms on the cable handrail as though just thoughtfully looking out over the river. But ever so stealthily, he reached over, peeled off the note Beth had taped there, thrust it into his pocket, and then ambled back up the bank.

Tears rolled down Caroline's cheeks. *She* wanted a note. *She* wanted romance. She didn't especially want Wally Hatford as a boyfriend, but if she had to have one to experience love, she'd do anything.

She went back to the house and lay facedown on the couch.

Mrs. Malloy looked in on her. "Tummy-ache, Caroline?" she asked.

Caroline rolled over on her back and stared at the ceiling. "Heartache," she replied in as tragic and dramatic a voice as she could manage.

Mrs. Malloy leaned against the doorway and studied her daughter. "Are we talking heartache as in a pain in the chest, or heartache as in a broken heart?" she asked.

"A broken heart," said Caroline. "Shattered into a million pieces." Oh, she was good. Even her mother believed her!

"Hmmm," said Mrs. Malloy. "We wouldn't be talking about one of the Hatford boys, would we? I thought we had an understanding that —"

"I don't want to talk about it," said Caroline, and turned her face to the wall. She felt so sorry for herself, she couldn't help smiling.

Dinner was early that evening because Mr. and Mrs. Malloy were attending a concert at the university.

"We won't be late, girls," their mother told them. "But I expect you to have your homework done and be in bed by the time we come back. Okay?"

"We will," Eddie promised.

The girls did watch TV for a while, however, but when they turned it off at eight-thirty and headed upstairs, all three of them saw it at the same time: an envelope thrust under the front door.

"Hey!" said Eddie. She bent down and picked it up.

" 'For My Beloved'?" she read aloud.

Caroline's heart leaped. From Wally. It *had* to be from Wally. "It's for me," she said, putting out her hand.

But Beth was reaching too. "No, it's for *me*," she said. "From Josh, obviously."

Eddie, however, was feeling playful, and she held the note high in the air where her sisters couldn't reach it.

"How do you know?" she said. *"Beloved* could be anyone. Maybe it's for *me!"* She took the note out of its envelope and held it over her head, then continued reading: " 'Dear Ugly Stupid . . .' "

Beth and Caroline both gasped.

"It doesn't say that, Eddie!" Beth cried. She leaped up and snatched the paper from Eddie's hand and turned her back to read it. And suddenly she threw it to the floor and, sobbing, ran upstairs and shut her door.

Eddie looked quizzically at Caroline. "Why would Josh write her a note like *that?"* she asked. "What a jerk!"

Caroline leaned down and picked up the piece of paper.

Dear Ugly Stupid,

You really are crazy, aren't you? I never liked you before, I don't like you now, and I won't like you in the future. Leave me alone.

Caroline gasped and clutched her chest, while Eddie stared. And then, just as Beth had done, she ran upstairs, gulping and sobbing, and shut *her* door. But as soon as she got inside, she stopped. Those sobs were so real! She really *was* a good actress. And then she had an idea. A wonderful, awful idea. She went to the phone in her parents' bedroom and dialed the Hatfords'.

Sixteen

Phone Call

With Mrs. Hatford working at the hardware store till nine and Mr. Hatford out bowling, Wally and Peter were at the kitchen table eating graham crackers and peanut butter when Josh came in and said, "Where's Jake?"

Wally shrugged. "I don't know. He had his coat on awhile ago. I thought you guys went somewhere."

"Well, he didn't tell me," Josh said.

There were sounds out in the hall, and Jake came in, his hair mussed up by the wind. He saw the snack on the table and helped himself to a big spoonful of peanut butter.

"Where have *you* been?" Josh asked him.

"Delivering a message to Caroline, that's what," Jake said, and told him about the valentine. Wally froze.

"Why would Caroline send a valentine to *you*?" Josh asked.

"Because she's crazy. She's out of her mind. She's as nutty as a PayDay candy bar," Jake answered.

Wally took another bite of cracker and pretended he was reading the label on the peanut butter jar. He hoped it might seem possible that a girl in fourth grade — a *precocious* girl who was only old enough for third — might be sending a stupid valentine to a boy in sixth grade.

"You mean she just walked up and handed you a mushy valentine?" Josh asked.

"She gave it to Wally to give to me."

Josh turned to Wally, and Wally swallowed. "Caroline handed you a valentine for Jake? Just like that?"

Wally swallowed again. "Just like that," he said. This was not the way he had planned things. In fact, he had not planned things at all. He had been so surprised by the envelope Caroline had handed him out in the hall at school that he had simply rushed for the door and thrust it at the first person he saw, who happened to be Jake. "For you," he had said. Which wasn't exactly the same as saying "Caroline said this was for you," so he hadn't really lied, had he? He sure didn't want his brothers to know that the card had been meant for *him!* He'd figured Jake would just take one glance at it and throw it out. Or maybe he'd throw it out without opening it at all.

Josh started to grin. "So what did you tell Caroline?" he asked Jake. "Are you going to carve your initials on a tree? Are you going to meet out on the bridge and kiss?" He seemed to enjoy teasing Jake, the way Jake had teased him.

Peter laughed too and swung his legs as he took a big drink of milk.

Jake glared at his twin. "*You* should talk! I know how you and Beth have been leaving notes for each other at the end of the bridge. You aren't any spy at all. You two are lovebirds, that's what."

"We are *not!*" Josh protested, his ears turning pink.

"Lovebirds! Lovebirds!" Jake chanted.

"We're not lovebirds! She's just a friend, and I find out all kinds of things from her," Josh said again.

"Like what?" Jake challenged. "That they're making something *gross* for us to eat? Yeah. Right!"

"Like how Eddie secretly wants to make pitcher on the baseball team at school."

"We know that already," said Jake.

"And how Caroline really likes Wally."

"She does not!" said Wally, but *his* ears gave him away. They were burning.

nds on the wooden planks of the idge. The four boys were panting when ey reached the top of the hill behind the Malloys' house. The back-porch light was n, and one of the cars was gone.

"I'll bet it's all a trick!" Jake said again. "Their folks are out for the evening, and Caroline's just trying to get even."

"Maybe," said Wally, and hoped his brother was right.

They hurried up the path to the back door, and then they stopped, one bumping into the other.

"Oh, no!" breathed Jake.

For there on the ground, on the crust of old snow, lay Caroline, her legs and arms at a strange angle, a pool of red beneath her head.

Both Jake and Josh turned on him then.

"I'll bet that valentine was for you!" Jake yelled. "I'll bet you knew it all the time! Caroline didn't write that card for me, did she?"

"I . . . I didn't say she did," Wally stammered. "I just gave it to you to get rid of it. I didn't know you were going to write her back."

"Wally!" yelled Jake and Josh together.

"Do you know what I just did?" Jake bellowed. "I stuck a note under their door."

"What did you say?" asked Josh.

"I wrote 'For My Beloved' on the outside, just the way she did. And on the inside I said, 'Dear Ugly Stupid, You really are crazy, aren't you? I never liked you before, I don't like you now, and I won't like you in the future. Leave me alone.'"

Wally swallowed. "You didn't sign it, did you?" he asked.

"No. I figured she'd just know."

Wally was almost relieved. He'd never have the nerve to be quite that rude, but if anything should stop Caroline from acting so weird, that note should do it. At that moment the phone rang and Wally reached around from his chair and answered. Somebody on the line was sobbing. "Who is this?" he asked.

But the sobbing grew louder still, and Wally knew it could only be Caroline Malloy.

"What's the matter?" he asked.

"H-How could you be so cruel?" she wept. "You don't have to love me, Wally, but you didn't have to call me ugly and stupid."

"It . . . it was —"

"You don't know how much that hurt!" Caroline continued.

"But . . . but I didn't write it. I gave it to —"

"Goodbye," said Caroline. "I'm just calling to tell you that you'll never have to look at my face again. You'll never have me sitting behind you in class or following you home from school again, because I will be dead. Goodbye, Wally. Forever!" And she hung up.

Wally stared at the phone in his hand and then at his brothers.

"Who was *that?*" asked Jake.

"C-Caroline, I . . . I think she's going to die," said Wally.

"*What?*" cried Josh.

Peter looked ready to cry.

"She's maybe going to kill herself," Wally said, scared.

"Because of my *note?*" asked Jake, disbelieving.

Wally nodded.

136

"She's got to be kidding!"

"I'm going over there and see."

"I'm going with you," said Jake.

"We'll all go," said Wally. "Put y on, Peter."

"We're not supposed to go over ever again!" Peter reminded them.

"Get your *coat!*" Josh ordered. "We leave you here alone."

"Wait a minute," said Jake. "If Caroli was going to do anything dumb like tha her sisters would stop her."

"Maybe they don't know," said Wally.

In a few seconds the boys had flung on their jackets and were racing down the hill to the swinging bridge.

"I still think it's a trick," said Jake. "You know how Caroline —"

"She was *sobbing!*" Wally insisted. "She said your note really hurt."

Peter stumbled on the untied laces of his sneakers, and the boys had to pull him back up onto his feet.

"Jake, you could go to jail if she dies," Wally said miserably. "You shouldn't have said what you did."

"Well, you shouldn't have given me that stupid valentine," said Jake. "If I go to jail, you'll go with me."

Their shoes made hollow thunking

137

Seventeen

More Trouble

This, Caroline thought, was her greatest performance yet. Even better than the abaguchie. Beth was upstairs in her room crying. Eddie was with her, telling her all the reasons the Hatfords were jerks. But *she* — Caroline Lenore Malloy — was lying out here with her legs tangled, her neck slightly twisted, and a knife clutched in her hand. And the Hatfords, all four of the Hatford boys, were standing over her, at least one of them, maybe two, making little gasping sounds. Peter, in fact, screamed.

"She *did* it!" came Jake's voice, scared. "My gosh, she really did it!"

"She did it out here so she wouldn't bleed all over the floor!" came Josh's hushed voice.

"Jake! We'll go to jail!" said Wally.

And then the sound of running feet, someone — probably Wally — running away.

Oh, this is wonderful! thought Caroline. Even better than she'd hoped. She had been afraid that when she dialed the Hatfords', one of the parents might answer. Or that Wally would say, "Yeah, right!" when she told him goodbye, and that no one would even bother to check.

But they had come, all four of the brothers. Wally had run away, she could see through half-closed eyes, but Peter was crying loudly, and one of the twins — Josh, she thought — was taking her pulse.

"I've got a pulse!" he cried. "She's alive! Call 911, somebody!"

A window opened upstairs. "Hey!" Eddie's voice. "What's going on? Caroline?"

"She's . . . she's hurt!" yelled Jake. "Call 911."

"*What?*" cried Eddie, and Beth appeared beside her at the window. "What are you guys doing over here? What's happened to Caroline?"

"I d-don't know!" Jake said.

The two girls disappeared from the window, and it seemed only seconds before they burst out the back door without their coats, crunching over the crusty snow and kneeling on the ground beside Caroline.

"Caroline?" Beth whimpered.

"She's . . . she's . . . ," Eddie began.

140

Both Jake and Josh turned on him then.

"I'll bet that valentine was for you!" Jake yelled. "I'll bet you knew it all the time! Caroline didn't write that card for me, did she?"

"I . . . I didn't say she did," Wally stammered. "I just gave it to you to get rid of it. I didn't know you were going to write her back."

"Wally!" yelled Jake and Josh together.

"Do you know what I just did?" Jake bellowed. "I stuck a note under their door."

"What did you say?" asked Josh.

"I wrote 'For My Beloved' on the outside, just the way she did. And on the inside I said, 'Dear Ugly Stupid, You really are crazy, aren't you? I never liked you before, I don't like you now, and I won't like you in the future. Leave me alone.' "

Wally swallowed. "You didn't sign it, did you?" he asked.

"No. I figured she'd just know."

Wally was almost relieved. He'd never have the nerve to be quite that rude, but if anything should stop Caroline from acting so weird, that note should do it. At that moment the phone rang and Wally reached around from his chair and answered. Somebody on the line was sobbing. "Who is this?" he asked.

But the sobbing grew louder still, and Wally knew it could only be Caroline Malloy.

"What's the matter?" he asked.

"H-How could you be so cruel?" she wept. "You don't have to love me, Wally, but you didn't have to call me ugly and stupid."

"It . . . it was —"

"You don't know how much that hurt!" Caroline continued.

"But . . . but I didn't write it. I gave it to —"

"Goodbye," said Caroline. "I'm just calling to tell you that you'll never have to look at my face again. You'll never have me sitting behind you in class or following you home from school again, because I will be dead. Goodbye, Wally. Forever!" And she hung up.

Wally stared at the phone in his hand and then at his brothers.

"Who was *that?*" asked Jake.

"C-Caroline, I . . . I think she's going to die," said Wally.

"*What?*" cried Josh.

Peter looked ready to cry.

"She's maybe going to kill herself," Wally said, scared.

"Because of my *note?*" asked Jake, disbelieving.

Wally nodded.

"She's got to be kidding!" said Josh. "I'm going over there and see."

"I'm going with you," said Jake.

"We'll all go," said Wally. "Put your coat on, Peter."

"We're not supposed to go over there ever again!" Peter reminded them.

"Get your *coat!*" Josh ordered. "We can't leave you here alone."

"Wait a minute," said Jake. "If Caroline was going to do anything dumb like that, her sisters would stop her."

"Maybe they don't know," said Wally.

In a few seconds the boys had flung on their jackets and were racing down the hill to the swinging bridge.

"I still think it's a trick," said Jake. "You know how Caroline —"

"She was *sobbing!*" Wally insisted. "She said your note really hurt."

Peter stumbled on the untied laces of his sneakers, and the boys had to pull him back up onto his feet.

"Jake, you could go to jail if she dies," Wally said miserably. "You shouldn't have said what you did."

"Well, you shouldn't have given me that stupid valentine," said Jake. "If I go to jail, you'll go with me."

Their shoes made hollow thunking

137

sounds on the wooden planks of the bridge. The four boys were panting when they reached the top of the hill behind the Malloys' house. The back-porch light was on, and one of the cars was gone.

"I'll bet it's all a trick!" Jake said again. "Their folks are out for the evening, and Caroline's just trying to get even."

"Maybe," said Wally, and hoped his brother was right.

They hurried up the path to the back door, and then they stopped, one bumping into the other.

"Oh, no!" breathed Jake.

For there on the ground, on the crust of old snow, lay Caroline, her legs and arms at a strange angle, a pool of red beneath her head.

Seventeen

More Trouble

This, Caroline thought, was her greatest performance yet. Even better than the abaguchie. Beth was upstairs in her room crying. Eddie was with her, telling her all the reasons the Hatfords were jerks. But *she* — Caroline Lenore Malloy — was lying out here with her legs tangled, her neck slightly twisted, and a knife clutched in her hand. And the Hatfords, all four of the Hatford boys, were standing over her, at least one of them, maybe two, making little gasping sounds. Peter, in fact, screamed.

"She *did* it!" came Jake's voice, scared. "My gosh, she really did it!"

"She did it out here so she wouldn't bleed all over the floor!" came Josh's hushed voice.

"Jake! We'll go to jail!" said Wally.

And then the sound of running feet, someone — probably Wally — running away.

Oh, this is wonderful! thought Caroline. Even better than she'd hoped. She had been afraid that when she dialed the Hatfords', one of the parents might answer. Or that Wally would say, "Yeah, right!" when she told him goodbye, and that no one would even bother to check.

But they had come, all four of the brothers. Wally had run away, she could see through half-closed eyes, but Peter was crying loudly, and one of the twins — Josh, she thought — was taking her pulse.

"I've got a pulse!" he cried. "She's alive! Call 911, somebody!"

A window opened upstairs. "Hey!" Eddie's voice. "What's going on? Caroline?"

"She's . . . she's hurt!" yelled Jake. "Call 911."

"*What?*" cried Eddie, and Beth appeared beside her at the window. "What are you guys doing over here? What's happened to Caroline?"

"I d-don't know!" Jake said.

The two girls disappeared from the window, and it seemed only seconds before they burst out the back door without their coats, crunching over the crusty snow and kneeling on the ground beside Caroline.

"Caroline?" Beth whimpered.

"She's . . . she's . . . ," Eddie began.

140

"Alive," Josh said. "I've got a pulse! Did someone call an ambulance?"

"What *happened?*" Beth asked accusingly.

"I thought . . . maybe she . . . well, sort of tried to kill herself," Jake said, pointing to the knife, and Beth screamed.

"Wait a minute," came Eddie's voice.

Uh-oh, thought Caroline. Through half-closed eyes she could see Eddie leaning close to her. She heard her sister sniff. Then she saw Eddie reach out with one finger, touch her head, then put the finger in her mouth.

"Raspberry syrup!" Eddie said, and jerked the knife out of her sister's hand. "Caroline, you creep, sit up!"

Instantly Caroline rolled over on her back and shrieked with laughter, clutching her chest.

"Caroline!" Jake said in disgust.

Eddie started to giggle, then Beth, and then the two older girls collapsed in laughter on the ground beside Caroline, while the boys looked on, embarrassed. All but Peter, who was so happy Caroline was alive that he piled on top of the girls, hooting with merriment.

"Man, oh man, did she ever trick *you!*" Eddie said, pointing to the guys.

"Well, she fooled you, too!" Josh said.

Beth turned on him. "Oh, what do you know about anything?" she snapped, suddenly jumping to her feet. "I don't know how you can stand there and face me, Josh Hatford, after that horrible note you sent."

"What?" cried Josh.

"So you thought I really liked you, didn't you? You thought I was your girlfriend. Well, how do you know I wasn't just using you to spy on you guys? How do you know I wasn't just being nice so you'd tell me what you were planning next?"

"*What?*" yelled Jake. "Josh, you didn't!"

"All that talk of how you guys were going to trick us this spring. All the things Jake said he'd do to make us miserable come summer. We know all your plans now, and that note you wrote didn't bother me a bit."

"*What* note?" asked Josh. "I didn't send you any note." He stared at Beth. Eddie and Caroline were staring too. "Do you mean the note Jake wrote to Caroline?"

Beth's mouth fell open. "That was for *Caroline?*"

"Why was Jake writing a note to *me?*" asked Caroline. "I thought Wally wrote it."

There was the sound of running feet below as Wally came tearing across the swinging bridge, and then, in the distance, a siren. Two sirens.

"Oh, no!" cried Josh, turning to face Wally, who came running back up the hill. "What did you do?"

"I ran home and called 911," said Wally, panting.

All seven of them looked at each other in horror as a patrol car came speeding across the road bridge at the end of Island Avenue and, with lights flashing and siren wailing, turned up the Malloys' drive.

Almost before it had stopped, two officers jumped out and came running over to the group.

"What's the problem here?" the first officer asked. "Where's the girl who was hurt?"

Caroline glanced around in dismay at the accusatory looks on the faces around her and tried to decide whether to admit it up front or faint for real.

"Is this the girl?" the officer asked, looking at the raspberry sauce that was drying on Caroline's cheek.

"That's her, and it was all a big joke!" Peter chortled, trying to be helpful.

The policeman looked at his partner and then back at Caroline. "Didn't we get a report not too long ago about a missing child who had been lured over here to see an abaguchie?"

An ambulance pulled up next, and the driver got out.

"Nobody's hurt," the policeman called. "Just kids horsing around."

The ambulance driver looked disgusted.

"What *is* it with you kids? You want to get arrested for turning in a false report?" asked the second officer.

Wally stepped forward. "I did it," he said, eager to have the whole mess over with. "I really thought she was hurt. I wasn't trying to trick you. I thought she tried to kill herself because of the note Jake wrote to her."

"You thought she'd kill herself over *Jake?*" Eddie screeched. "Get real!"

The officer focused on Caroline again. "What's with the raspberry syrup?"

"It's supposed to be blood, I think," Peter said importantly.

"Peter, will you shut up?" said Jake between his teeth.

Caroline dramatically pulled herself to her feet. "I'm responsible for the whole thing," she said. "Arrest me."

The officer cocked his head. "Well, now, I'd like to, but simple aggravation isn't quite enough to do it. What made you do a

144

fool stunt like this?"

"Unrequited love," said Caroline.

The two officers suddenly started to laugh. So did the ambulance driver.

Well, let them, Caroline told herself. She had now experienced heartbreak and rejection, and though she could not officially add romance to the list, no one could say she was boring.

"Tell you what," one of the policemen said, "if you kids can't find enough to do, there are a lot of things that need doing down at police headquarters. You can stop in anytime and scrub our floor, empty wastebaskets, sweep the steps, clean the toilets . . . How about it? Think you can find enough to do to keep out of trouble, or do you want to come down to headquarters a couple afternoons a week and clean up?"

"I . . . I think we can stay out of trouble," Wally said quickly. The others nodded.

More headlights turned in at the end of the drive, and Mr. Hatford jumped out of his Jeep. "I was bowling, and picked up a radio call on my police band," he said. "Is one of the Malloy girls hurt?"

"Just a little raspberries on the brain," the second officer said as the two policemen walked toward their car and the ambulance driver turned around in the clearing. "Sorry to have interrupted your game, Tom."

There were still more headlights turning in, the ones Caroline dreaded most: her parents car returning home.

Mrs. Malloy almost fell out of the car in her haste to see what was wrong.

"Eddie! What . . . ?" she cried, rushing over.

"Everything's okay, Mom. A misunderstanding, that's all. Nobody's hurt and everyone's leaving."

"Including us," said Wally, turning.

"Hold it right there," bellowed his father. "I thought we specifically asked you boys to stay on the other side of the river. Why didn't you?"

"Because Caroline called us," said Wally.

"She said she was dying," put in Peter.

"Caroline!" said her father. "I told you girls not to bother the boys anymore. What's going on?"

"I had to call because of the note. Beth was crying," Caroline answered.

"What note?" asked her father.

"The note Jake sent me."

"Why was Beth crying?"

"She thought it was from Josh."

"Why did Jake send a note to you?"

"He thought the valentine was for him."

"What valentine?"

"The valentine I sent Wally."

"Well, you folks sort it out. Unrequited love is too complicated for us," said the first officer, as the men got into their patrol car. "Good night."

Mr. Hatford looked at his sons. "Home!" he ordered, and the four boys retreated down the hill. He got into his Jeep, backed out of the driveway, and headed across the road bridge.

Coach Malloy glared at his daughters. "House!" he said, pointing. The three girls went inside, followed by their parents.

Caroline was frightened. Her father, his face purple red, looked as though he might explode.

"George, let me handle this," said Mrs. Malloy.

"You'd better, because if the police show up here one more time, I'm going to *give* those girls away!" he bellowed, and went marching up the stairs, each step sounding like thunder.

Mrs. Malloy herded the girls into the dining room. "Sit!" she ordered.

Caroline fell weakly into a chair at the head of the table. Mrs. Malloy sat at the other end, and Beth and Eddie sat together on one side.

"Tell me *everything!*" the girls' mother commanded. "Don't leave out a single thing."

Timidly Caroline began. All the things she had done to get Wally to fall in love with her, how he'd rejected her valentine, her phone call to the Hatfords, the death scene with the raspberry syrup . . . Every now and then Beth or Eddie would chime in with a detail she had overlooked. Then Mrs. Malloy asked questions of her two older daughters — exactly how the Hatford boys had been involved in the science project, whether Beth considered Josh her boyfriend . . .

When all had been told, Mrs. Malloy simply sat with her hands folded under her chin and surveyed her daughters. Mrs. Malloy quiet was even more alarming than Mrs. Malloy angry.

"I thought," said Mrs. Malloy finally, looking first at Caroline, "that you wanted to be an actress. A very good actress."

Caroline stared. "I *do!* That's what this was all about!"

"No," said her mother. "That is not what it was all about. What it was about was making Wally Hatford as uncomfortable as possible. What it was about was embarrassing those boys. The first thing a really good actress must have is the ability to empathize with other people. Do you know what that means, Caroline?"

"I . . . I'm not sure," Caroline murmured.

"It means thinking what they're thinking, feeling what they're feeling, and then showing that you care."

Caroline sniffled.

"If you embarrassed Wally in front of your class and again after he called the police, and felt nothing for what *he* must be feeling," Mrs. Malloy went on, "then I would say you have no empathy at all, Caroline, and you'd better choose another career."

Caroline's eyes immediately filled with tears. "I . . . I . . . *did* understand what he was feeling, but —"

"But you didn't *care?* That's even worse, Caroline."

Caroline was sobbing now. "I *do* want to be an actress. More than anything in the world. Oh, I *do*, Mother, I do!" Beth and Eddie were staring at her uncomfortably, but Caroline was desperate to make her mother understand.

"So are those real tears or make-believe?

I can't even tell anymore," Mrs. Malloy said with disgust in her voice. "I am very disappointed in you, Caroline."

"I'll . . . I'll make it up to Wally!" Caroline pleaded. "I'll write him a note —"

"*No!*" said Beth and Eddie together.

"No more notes," said Beth. "I've seen enough notes to last a lifetime."

"I'll . . . I'll call him up," said Caroline.

"No more phone calls," said her mother. "Tomorrow you will walk right up to Wally Hatford and tell him you are sorry. Do you understand me, Caroline?"

Caroline nodded, still weeping.

Mrs. Malloy turned to Eddie next. "*You* will apologize to the Hatfords for tricking Josh and Jake into a science project they didn't completely understand." Then she looked at Beth. "I don't know what *you'll* apologize for, but I'll think of something. Do you two girls understand me?"

"Yes," said Eddie and Beth together in small voices.

"Go to bed," said their mother.

The girls went upstairs. The lights in the Malloy house began to go out, one by one. Finally all the windows were dark and there was nothing left but two shining eyes, like hot burning coals, watching from the trees in back of the house.

Eighteen

Secret Meetings

Jake, Josh, Wally, and Peter beat their father home on foot, but they didn't get upstairs before his Jeep pulled into the driveway and he stormed into the house.

"What did we *tell* you?" he yelled, lining them up like soldiers before a firing squad. "What did we say about going across the bridge and hanging around the Malloys?"

"We *had* to, Dad! We thought she was dying! She called and said goodbye — that we'd never see her again," Wally explained. He usually let his brothers answer for him if he could, but he figured he was dead no matter what, so why not come right out with it?

"How could she be dying if she called you on the phone?" Mr. Hatford asked.

"We thought she was going to shoot herself or something," said Jake.

"So you just *had* to go over there and get

151

involved in the prank, didn't you? Haven't you guys learned anything at all?"

"I guess so," said Josh. "We learned that when somebody says they're going to kill themselves, never take it seriously."

Mr. Hatford blinked.

"Yeah," added Jake. "We learned that no matter how much somebody needs you, never get involved because it might get you in trouble."

"Now, wait a minute. You could have called 911 without ever going over there," said their father.

"Is that what you want us to do?" asked Wally. "Whenever the Whomper, the Weirdo, or the Crazie calls, and says she's dying or something, we should just pick up the phone and dial the police without even going over to check? Would that be any better?"

Mr. Hatford closed his eyes. "Oh, how I wish the Bensons were back. I know that a pack of boys can get into mischief too, but I never knew that boys and girls together could cause such a ruckus."

The boys exchanged glances, sensing they were winning.

"Look at it this way, Dad. We may make mistakes, but at least we're trying to be good citizens," Josh told him.

"All right, but I repeat," said their father wearily, "don't cross the river unless it's absolutely necessary. And for heaven's sake, don't let your mother find out what happened tonight."

The clock struck nine, and Peter had just started up the stairs when Mrs. Hatford's car pulled into the driveway. Twenty seconds later she was coming through the kitchen like a tornado, saying, "What in the world happened tonight? I got calls at the hardware store, Wally, saying that you dialed 911, but when I called home there was no answer. What's going on?" She tossed her keys on the coffee table and looked around the living room.

"Don't ask," said her husband.

"Just tell me this: Are the Malloys involved again?" Mrs. Hatford stared right at Wally.

This always happens, he thought. With four sons to choose from, why did she always end up directing her questions to him?

But Peter answered for him from the stairs. He leaned over the banister and called, "Caroline said she was dying and we went over to watch."

"What?" cried Mrs. Hatford. "To *watch?*"

"It was a false alarm," said Wally. "Nobody died. Caroline just got a little raspberry syrup in her hair, that's all."

"*What?*" his mother said again. "You called 911 for that?"

"Ellen," said her husband, "trust me. The more you ask, the more confused you will get. Let's just hope that the Malloys go back to Ohio come summer, the Bensons return, and we have only to deal with the insanity of nine boys."

"That's fine with me," she told him. "It's been a difficult day at the hardware store, and I don't need anything else to worry about. Peter, go take your bath."

The boys scattered, and Wally breathed a sigh of relief that for now, anyway, the worst was over. Later, as he picked up the comics from the coffee table, he saw that a letter had come from Georgia. He took it up to his room to read.

Dear Wally (and Jake and Josh and Peter),

All the excitement must be going on in West Virginia right now, because there isn't a lot going on down here, and we're really missing you guys.

Dad's talking about maybe taking a job in

Macon, but he hasn't decided yet, and I think if I don't see snow again, I'll go nuts. All we get is ice. Georgia's okay, but it's all what you're used to, I guess, and I sure miss the hills. We all do, even Mom. We had some great times, didn't we?

What are the Malloy girls up to these days? Man, they must really keep you guessing. We could do with a little adventure down here right now. Any chance the Whomper, the Weirdo, and the Crazie might come here?

> *Bill (and Danny and Steve and Tony and Doug)*

When the Hatford boys set off for school the next day, the three Malloy girls were waiting at the end of the bridge.

"Well, you survived," Jake remarked.

"Yeah, but boy, was Mom mad!" said Eddie. "And Dad was practically ballistic. So we have to apologize."

"Yeah? For what?" asked Jake.

"Well, for not leveling with you about the science project, for one thing. And for what we put you through yesterday. Caroline was being a jerk, and we should have throttled her instead of laughing about it."

Beth looked at Josh. "And I'm sorry about all that stuff I said yesterday."

"Was it true, though? You were really just spying?" he asked.

"No. I wasn't spying at all, but I don't think I want to be your girlfriend anymore. It's too confusing."

"Aha!" said Jake. "So she *was!*"

"We'll just be friends, right?" said Josh, and Beth nodded.

"And now that I know what it is like to have loved and lost, Wally, so that if I ever have to play it on Broadway, I can do it from the heart, you don't have to be my boyfriend anymore either," Caroline said.

"I never *was* your boyfriend!" Wally yelped.

"Caroline!" warned her sisters.

Caroline took a deep breath. "And I am honestly, truly, profoundly, deeply, intensely sorry for giving you a mushy valentine and embarrassing you in front of the class and pretending I was dead," she said. She got down on one knee. "And I humbly, sincerely, honestly ask your forgiveness, now and forever."

"Caroline!" her sisters said again.

Caroline got up and brushed off the knees of her pants. "But we still aren't supposed to cross the bridge except when we're going to school," she told them.

"And we can't come over to Island Avenue unless it's a real emergency, and you know what will happen if we turn in a false alarm again," Josh said.

"We'll have to clean toilets!" said Peter grimly.

"So what are we going to do for fun around here?" Beth wondered as they all set off for school.

"We'll just have to meet at other places," said Josh. "How about Oldakers' Bookstore?"

"Deal!" said Eddie. "Mom didn't say we couldn't go downtown anymore. Let's meet there after dinner tonight."

It was a whole new way of doing things, Wally thought. Nobody was calling anyone names. No one was dumping dead birds and squirrels on the other side of the river, and no one was trying to steal his underpants. Were they actually *friends* now — friends the way the Hatfords used to be with the Bensons?

That evening after dinner, all four boys got permission to walk downtown as long as they had their homework done and were in bed by nine-thirty.

The Malloy girls were already at the

bookstore when they arrived, looking through paperbacks that had just been stocked in the mystery section. Beth's nose was deep in a book on vampires.

They were all sitting around on the floor, talking about what they could do together in Buckman when the weather got warmer, when two women burst into the bookstore with news that the abaguchie had been sighted loping along the alley behind the store. The police were asking everyone to stay inside.

Nineteen

Abaguchie

Next to lying on the ground with her head in a pool of raspberry syrup, this was one of the most exciting things that had ever happened to her, Caroline decided. She and her sisters were trapped with the Hatford boys inside Oldakers' Bookstore while the police and sheriff were prowling the streets and alleys looking for the creature that had been in the news for the past few months, eluding everyone.

"Stay right where you are till your father comes to get you," Mrs. Malloy said when Caroline called home to say where they were.

"Don't even think about stepping out of that store till your dad says it's safe," Mrs. Hatford said when Wally phoned her.

So the Hatford boys and the Malloy girls crowded around the door of the bookstore, watching all the activity outside and wondering what kind of animal the abaguchie really was.

"What do you suppose it eats for dinner?" Peter asked, his eyes wide, as a policeman walked by the front window.

"Second-grade boys, what else?" joked Eddie. "Starts with the ears and saves the toes for dessert."

"Naw," said Jake. "I think it goes for girls. *Precocious* girls, because it enjoys listening to them squeal when it nibbles their fingers."

"Hey, Caroline!" said Josh. "You can never be a really good actress unless you've experienced genuine terror. How about going outside and checking the alley? See if it's safe to leave?"

"Nobody leaves this store until your folks come for you," called Mike Oldaker, the owner, which made it more exciting still.

As it turned out, the abaguchie outsmarted them all again. Despite the number of officers who were out looking for the animal, it was nowhere to be found. Coach Malloy came for his daughters, Tom Hatford came for his sons, and Oldakers' Bookstore closed early.

A few days later, the newspaper carried another story:

ABAGUCHIE FOUND TO BE COUGAR, the headline read. And it told how the high-school biology teacher had heard his dog bark and had gone out in the yard to find his pet in the jaws of a cougar, which, startled by a yell from the teacher, dropped its prey and disappeared into the woods. The dog, fortunately, lived to wag his tail again.

The animal was definitely a cougar, the teacher said, and residents were warned to go outside only in groups, especially children walking to and from school.

"George!" Mrs. Malloy cried at breakfast. "This is serious! I'm not even sure Caroline is safe when she's with her sisters. A cougar is a mountain lion, you know. It always goes after the smallest and weakest member of the crowd."

Eddie, who wasn't much afraid of anything, went on eating her toast. "Just make sure we're always walking with the Hatfords, then," she said dryly. "If the cougar spots us, it'll take Peter."

"Edith Ann!" her mother said.

But Coach Malloy put down his fork. "You know, Jean, that's not a bad idea."

"*What?* Using little Peter for bait?" Mrs. Malloy cried.

"No, sticking with a larger crowd. The more kids there are walking together, the less chance any of them will be attacked." He looked around the table. "Why don't you girls make it a point to walk with the Hatfords to school and back each day? In fact, it's fine with me if they walk you all the way home."

Beth and Eddie and Caroline exchanged glances. Was this turning out well, or what?

So when the girls reached the end of the swinging bridge later, the boys were waiting.

"Mom said we have to wait for you every morning," Josh said, smiling. "She wants us all to stay together and keep an eye on Peter — not let him lag behind or anything."

"Same with us," said Beth. "We have to keep an eye on Caroline."

"So we have to stick together whether we want to or not!" said Wally.

"Yeah, as long as you stay in Buckman, you have to stick to us like glue." Jake grinned. "You have to follow us wherever we go: down the old coal mine, along Smuggler's Cove, through the woods, up the mountain . . ."

"You think we're chicken?" asked Eddie. "You think we're scared? Just wait! You haven't seen anything yet!"

▼

About the Author

Phyllis Reynolds Naylor enjoys writing about the Hatford boys and the Malloy girls because the books take place in her husband's home state, West Virginia. The town of Buckman in the stories is really Buckhannon, where her husband spent most of his growing-up years. Mrs. Naylor plans to write one book for each month that the girls are in Buckman, though who knows whether or not they will move back to Ohio at the end?

Phyllis Reynolds Naylor is the author of more than a hundred books, a number of which are set in West Virginia, including the Newbery Award–winning *Shiloh* and the other two books in the Shiloh trilogy, *Shiloh Season* and *Saving Shiloh*. She and her husband live in Bethesda, Maryland.

The employees of Thorndike Press hope you have enjoyed this Large Print book. All our Thorndike and Wheeler Large Print titles are designed for easy reading, and all our books are made to last. Other Thorndike Press Large Print books are available at your library, through selected bookstores, or directly from us.

For information about titles, please call:

(800) 223-1244

or visit our Web site at:

www.gale.com/thorndike
www.gale.com/wheeler

To share your comments, please write:

Publisher
Thorndike Press
295 Kennedy Memorial Drive
Waterville, ME   04901